Award-winning, Amazon Bestselling author Steven Paul Leiva is your tour guide to some of the strange destinations he has visited through the years.

In *Made on the Moon,* travel with Leiva into the mind of one Stanley Lewis, a little man with a big dream. He had wanted to go to the Moon since he was an infant..

Then go even deeper into Stanley's mind as Leiva takes you to the poetic realm of this little man's brain by presenting *What a Pleasure it's Been to Piss in Porcelain: The Rude Poems of Stanley Lewis.* As you might guess, you don't want to read these poems to your mother.

Next stop—Mars! We are joined on the tour by Cyrano De Bergerac and Baron Munchausen in the year 1641. Although the Baron is actually from 1790. A weird situation for historical personages. But then Cyrano and the Baron were also fictional characters. An imaginative tale about real imaginative gentlemen on a surreal trip tripping over the real.

Then two short stops to conclude our voyages. You won't even need an overnight bag.

EXTRAORDINARY VOYAGES

EXTRAORDINARY VOYAGES

Your Itinerary

MADE ON THE MOON
A Novella

CYRANO DE BERGERAC AND
BARON MUNCHAUSEN
GO TO MARS
A Short Story

And Some Other Places including

WHAT A PLEASURE IT'S BEEN
TO PISS IN PORCELAIN
The Rude Poems of Stanley Lewis

Your Tour Guide

StevenPaul Leiva

Magpie

Press

"Steven Leiva not only promises but delivers. Bravo!" — Ray Bradbury

Praise for *Made on the Moon: A Novella*

"With just enough satirical elements to emphasize the blurred line between logic and insanity, true fans of Science Fiction will find a kindred attachment with the Stanley Lewis character." — **Ricky L. Brown,** *Amazing Stories Magazine*

"Leiva has crafted a satire with a very warm heart...you'll love every page." — **Russell Blackford, author of** *Science Fiction and the Moral Imagination.*

"Brisk and touching comic novel...Highly recommended!" — **John Billingsley, "Dr. Phlox" on** *Star Trek Enterprise* **and a voracious reader.**

Praise for the Fiction of Steven Paul Leiva

"*Traveling in Space's* humor and refreshing perspective are thoroughly enjoyable" — **Diane Ackerman, New York Times bestselling author of** *The Zookeeper's Wife*

"*Journey to Where* impressively showcases author Steven Paul Leiva's genuine flair for originality and a distinctive, reader-engaging narrative storytelling style." — *Midwest Book Review*

"*Creature Feature* is a weird, funny, twisty romp...highly entertaining and highly recommended." — **Jonathan Maberry, NY Times bestselling author of** *Rot & Ruin* **and** *V-Wars*

DESTINATIONS

MADE ON THE MOON

A Novella

Made on the Moon was originally published as a stand-alone novella by Crossroad Press in 2017. It had had a long journey starting in the 1970s. I outline that journey in "From Stage to Page—The Phases of Made on the Moon" later in this book. This version has been slightly revised from the 2017 edition.

STEVEN PAUL LEIVA

1

Within the desolation, the facility rests, functioning as designed, alive with controlled activity, much of it repetitive, day-to-day, stretching on for years.

Many come, few leave, careers are made here, careers end here.

Gray is the color scheme, gray is often the mood, walls surround, outside is non-existent.

Visitors are few, but when they come, they come with purpose. They are given sparse rooms to sleep in and the interrogation room to conduct their business in.

Three are here now—anxious, excited, wondering. One male of a mixed heritage of many parts; two females, one older, one younger, both of superior intelligence. But they are not as intelligent, the mixed-heritage male thinks, as he himself. Which is why he thinks he is the leader.

They have been in the gray interrogation room all day, with but one break for a short lunch of uninspiring facility food, tasteless bureaucratic bites chewed automatically and quickly engaging three mouths tired from asking questions of individual after individual after individual, whom, if they were to think back on them, they could not visually distinguish, could not see their faces, could only see their files and the new notes they have entered in them.

The three interviewers, who cannot be named within the facility for rational reasons, all wear identical, facility-issued jumpsuits of, oddly, powder blue. It is to distinguish them from the administrators of the facility who wear jumpsuits of red, and the facility residents who wear jumpsuits of a sickly green. They sit side-by-side-by-side at a long gray table.

The mixed-heritage male is forty-two years of age and has worked hard to look distinguished, an effect somewhat diminished by the jumpsuit. He has a large dark blue R stitched onto the left side of his chest area.

The older woman is fifty-five, slim, a handsome woman now that pretty has left her. She has a large dark blue S stitched onto the jumpsuit over her small and useless left breast.

The younger woman is probably older than the twenty-four years she looks, which is not that unusual. She has a large dark blue T curving over her ample, vibrant left breast.

Their last interviewee has just left, and they all take a breath, some sips of facility water, and a moment's reflection.

R breaks the moment by asking, "Who's next?"

S consults a file and names the name, "Stanley Lewis."

"Born?" R asks.

"1949," S announces.

"Really? Let me see?" R reaches for the file, and S hands it to him. Reluctantly? It seems so. She is the keeper of the files and has a certain territorial sense of possession.

R looks over the file. "Hmm," he finally says. "If ever the term nondescript applied...not much of an adventurer, was he?" R gives the file one last scan, maybe in the hope of finding a shiny nugget, but nothing glints. "It's getting late. We have three likely candidates. Why don't we call it quits here?"

"He's the last to be interviewed," T reminds or possibly informs. In either case, R is not happy to have his idea challenged.

"Yes, I'm well aware of that. But as we have three likely candidates, I see no reason to prolong the day."

"I'm not happy with the three," T says.

"Oh, you're not? Well, I am."

"And you are the leader of the team."

"And I am the leader of the team."

"May *I* see?" T stretches out her arm across the front of S and holds out her hand to R for the file marked "Stanley Lewis." R reluctantly hands the file to T, who withdraws it past the front of S, claiming it for her own. She looks it over, reading quickly, flipping pages with sharp, brittle crinkle sounds that irritate R. "He has led a life," T reports her assessment. "He has lived to this age. How much of an adventurer do you need?"

"It is important to note," S says, being between R and T and forced to mediate, "that each one of the three likely candidates has a drawback, as we have all discussed. Can we afford not to find a more perfect one?"

R stares at S and T; S and T stare right back.

"It's not really that late," S says.

"It is always *that* late," R declares what for him is a universal truth. But the weight of that truth does not fall on S and T, who continue to stare at R, occasionally blinking, the blinks being like little, sharp pokes at the center of his forehead. "All right, yes, yes, of course, you're right. Well then, let us talk to, uh…." He reaches out for the file, and it travels from T, past S, to him, and he glances at it. "…Stanley Lewis."

+

A description of the nondescript: Short, no taller than five foot five, thin, possibly not a big eater, pallid, but that could be a result of the sickly green jumpsuit he wears. He has mandatory close-cropped gray hair and a well-shaved-by-decree face, and yet somehow, it looks grizzled. His eyes are focused on something no one else can see, and his discontent is too prominent for his own good.

Stanley Lewis paces in a small space. Back and forth. Back and forth. Back and forth. Inches become feet become yards become miles—or kilometers if you must make your way metrically—become infinity, which is the same for everyone.

A man in a red jumpsuit sits on a chair, feeling cramped. He is waiting for a communication to voice in the implant in his ear that will tell him to deliver Stanley Lewis to the interrogation room. He has only been here since he delivered the last sickly green jumpsuited resident to the powder blue visitors. But already is bored listening to Stanley Lewis talk and talk rapidly to no one in particular. Or to everyone in general. Wanting to get it out, wanting it to be noted.

"I was born during a full moon, and its deflected sunlight filled me with my being and offered me more succor than my own mother, who, soon after my birth, took me away from her breast as my teeth came in early and my instinct was to bite."

Stanley stops pacing and calls the man's attention to a history playing out before him but invisible to the man in the red jumpsuit. "Oh, look, look, look, there she sits, with the infant me, on the front lawn. She is communing with the cool night air and holds the infant me and feeds the infant me from a bottle that she has screwed into the infant me's mouth in order to bring a little, a little, well—peace on Earth."

Stanley starts to pace again but never takes his eyes off of mother and child.

"Look, look, look, the infant me reaches up with hands wanting to grasp. All infants do that. But this infant me is not reaching up to stroke his mother's face, this infant me is not reaching up to play with some bauble hanging from her neck. No, no, no, this infant me is reaching up to that white, bright illumination that hung high in the sky above his mother. God. *His* God." Stanley stops and turns and stares at the man in the red jumpsuit with fear, yet determination, with hesitancy, yet aggression, and tells him that,

"You can't have him!"

The man in the red jumpsuit is not surprised by this declaration; he may well have heard it before, and he makes no acknowledgment that it has even been stated. That satisfies Stanley Lewis, who returns to his pacing.

"When the infant me became the child me and the child me could stand, the child me stood out on the front lawn—then fell straight back…."

Stanley Lewis falls straight back, and the man jumps up in his red jumpsuit to catch him, which he does then lowers him down to lay on the floor. With a chuckle and a shake of his head, the man returns to his chair while Stanley continues.

"…to look straight up at the white light at its zenith. It was then that the child me first saw the face. And the child me felt unbalanced, floating, flat up against the sky facing the very old friendly face of the Man in the Moon directly, addressing him on his terms—a body in space."

Stanley Lewis stands up and twirls a rotation or two or three, then falls to sit on the only other chair in the room.

"Ah, look, later, the little boy me no longer lays on the grass, he sits, sits on the lawn chair and looks up at the moon with stronger eyes, more powerful eyes—his dad's inexpensive pair of field binoculars made to see up close the movements of birds and animals, enemy agents, and divorcees with open blinds. But used by the little boy me to view his old god, his friend, his moon."

Stanley looks up and circles his two thumbs and index

fingers, and puts them to his eyes.

"And what the little boy me saw astounded! Not a white light, a spot, a disk with a friendly face at all. But a place, a sphere with rounding edges returning, covered with craters, the beauty marks of the moon, the distinction that made the moon so otherworldly, so unearthly. A place, the little boy me realized, a place you could go to. And why not? The infant me, the child me, the little boy me was born on the Earth. But must we always end where we start? Must we? You see, the me—the me had always wanted to go to the moon."

Stanley slowly turns his attention to the man in the red jumpsuit and declares to him:

"I had wanted to go to the moon from the time I was an infant."

The man in the red jumpsuit makes no acknowledgment of Stanley's monumental statement but does acknowledge a voice in his ear. "Okay, will do," he says to someone who is not there as he gestures for Stanley to stand.

+

R and S and T sit silently at their long, gray table. They are done talking to each other, and each indulges in the delights of their own minds. The door to the interview room opens, and the man in the red jumpsuit leads Stanley Lewis in, leaving him standing in the middle of a room by a gray metal, shyly utilitarian chair.

"Please be seated, Mr. Lewis," S says, a kindly smile on her lips.

Stanley takes a moment to do so, wondering why—although it hardly matters.

"Mr. Lewis, you have been told to cooperate with us," T says, following the script she has followed all day, "and we expect that cooperation. We will be asking you—"

"Why are you here?" Stanley interrupts.

No one has interrupted before. Some have stared, some have sneered, some have scoffed, but no one has interrupted before. "Uh, we are here to learn—"

"You expect me to teach?"

"Well…," S consults Stanley's file, now back with her. "You once were a teacher, weren't you? So, yes, teach us."

"I was a lousy teacher."

"Well—," T begins.

"I hated my students."

"Well—," T tries again.

"I can only inform."

"Inform us then," S requests with a smile and commands with a stare.

"Of what?"

"Of why you are—"

"I had wanted to go to the moon from the time I was an infant."

"Now, Mr. Lewis," S says as kindly as she can, "there is no reason to be facetious."

"Facetious?"

"Mr. Lewis, we are conducting—"

"You asked me to inform. It is the only thing I have to inform you of."

T, wanting to move forward to finish this long day, says, "Okay, Mr. Lewis, however you want to inform us."

"No!" R has been growing increasingly frustrated and angered by the incompetence of his colleagues. He decides to put an end to it. "This is certainly not germane to our purpose here. What we want, Mr. Lewis, is for you to tell us some particulars about your life, starting with your child-hood."

Stanley looks at R. *I don't like you*, he thinks, *you're a bully.* "That's all in the files," he says flatly.

"Facts are in the files, Mr. Lewis," T explains the subtle-ty. "We are trying to get at the truth."

Trumpets blare. No one is aware of them but Stanley. "Oh. The truth!"

"We haven't even read your file," S lies.

"You haven't?" Lewis is astounded.

"No, not really," S qualifies the lie. "Just glanced at it. We are trying to approach this fresh."

Fresh, hell, R thinks, *there's nothing fresh about this old fart.* He condescends to address Stanley in a condescending man-ner, "Let me see if I can help you along, Mr. Lewis. Why don't you tell us about your happiest days as a child, your most precious memories."

Happiest days? Stanley thinks. He closes his eyes as if to shut out now. *Precious memories?* Stanley smiles and opens his eyes, and looks right at R. "Well, there was the summer my father bought the used '55 Caddy with the automatic windows and seats."

A breakthrough! T rejoices. She leans toward Stanley and becomes the personification of encouragement. "Yes? Was that a particularly memorable summer?"

"Sure. It was the summer my mother became our small town's one and only piano teacher. And the summer my sister turned sixteen and learned what it was to become a woman. That summer, that summer of hot, lazy days punctuated by now and then celebrations of life, that's the childhood summer I now remember with the most affection. That's the one I would most like to return to."

"Good!" S says. "Do that for us. Relive that summer. Take us there."

Stanley looks up as if the past is floating somewhere above him, and closes his eyes, and sees…

His small town. Beautiful in bucolic surroundings. One main street, several branching streets, one particular street.

"We lived on Pinewood Avenue, a broad, tree-shaded street of long lawns and two-story clapboard houses containing families that each had their own distinctive tune, with harmonies of pleasure or discords of pain, as if each family was a song. For example, the Andersons were a Vaudeville ditty."

The Andersons are cheerfully shopping downtown. Dad in his bowler and ever-present cigar; Mom beautifully dressed as if every day was Sunday; Little Mary Sunshine, their daughter, the delight of their lives. Sam, across the street, big man in town; owns property and dictates propriety, yells out in greeting and crosses the road with his hand already extended, "Hey Andersons, how you all doing?"

"What?" Mr. Anderson says, confused until he sees Sam heading his way. "Oh, Hi, Sam. How you doing?"

Sam's big, beefy hand locks onto Mr. Anderson's glad hand. "Never better, never better! Hey you old dog, you, you gonna MC the Elks dinner again this year?"

"Sure, sure. Got all new jokes. Went up to the big city last summer, caught all the shows, got a whole slew of new jokes! And, look-look-look here, Martha's going to do a re-ci-ta-tion. Tell him what you're going to do, Mother."

"Oh," Martha giggles and demurs and shyly looks down, "it's just a little poem by Oscar Wilde. I hope people won't think it's too bold."

"No, no, Mother, it'll be fine, it'll be fine. And listen, listen, Little Mary Sunshine here is going to do a dance."

And Little Mary Sunshine jumps into her dance for a few steps announcing, "I made it up all by myself!"

"Yep," the proud father says. "So make sure you come, Sam. Never a dull moment when the Andersons are on the stage."

Stanley chuckles in fond memory. Then his mouth turns down, and he opens sad eyes to tell R and S and T that, "Now, on the other hand, the Brisbanes were a dirge.

Huddled in their tiny apartment over their grocery store, the Brisbanes spend their evenings consoling each other.

"Three sons lost in the war," Mr. Brisbane says, still trying to grasp the fact. "And little Dotty dead from leukemia." As he has often in the past, he reaches out to Mrs. Brisbane.

"Yes, Henry, we've had our tragedies. But we still have our Tom."

Husband and wife; father and mother, look to Tom—twelve-year-old Tom, the hope of their future.

"And I'll make you proud of me, Mom and Dad. I'll make you proud enough for ten children. By gosh, you just see if I don't!"

The three grab each other—and hang on for dear life.

"Oddly enough," Stanley tells S because somehow he thinks S will understand, "the two families, the Andersons and the Brisbanes, they were the best of friends. It was as if they needed each other to balance their lives."

S thinks this is telling.

T thinks this is interesting.

R thinks this is boring.

"Now, the Fords...Well, the Fords were a romantic ballad."

Damn attractive young couple, the Fords. People liked being in their company whenever they were in town, which they often weren't, as they were always off on one adventure after another. But when they were home, they held court at the one nice restaurant in the one hotel in the town and told their story again.

"He was a roving adventurer, tall and handsome, with a wide-open and friendly you-can-count-on-me face," Mrs. Ford would start.

"She was a foreign correspondent assigned to write glamorous articles to match her glamorous self," Mr. Ford would continue.

"We met one day in Marrakech."

"Married the next day in Paris,"

"Honeymooned in Tibet."

"We've roamed the world together."

"But we always come back to this—"

"Our small town—"

"The birthplace of us both."

"And what about your family," S asks Stanley.

"My family? Why—we were a symphony!"

In the house of his childhood—two-story with a fine big attic and a cavernous basement lived...

"Dad, he was the mellow bassoons."

And...

"Mom, Mom was the sweet violins."

And...

"Sis—well, Sis was the piano. With many mysterious keys to herself."

"And what about you, Mr. Lewis?"

"Me? I was the...

"PERCUSSION INSTRUMENTS!" his family says in unison as they hover around Stanley.

"Loud," His sis says.

"Getting into everything," his mom says.

"Always wanting to be heard," his dad shakes his head, yet smiles in remembering.

"Oh, Lordy, yes, you were loud!" His mom chuckles as she exclaims.

"Was I really, Mom? Was I really that loud?"

"Loud enough to wake the devil himself!"

"Dad, was I really?"

"Got you into a lot of trouble now and then. Had to take the strap to you on occasion. But that wasn't often."

"It was just youthful energy, son."

"Yes, it was basically good energy coming from a good boy."

"Except when I tried to have a boyfriend over. I couldn't sit on the front porch with any boy without a firecracker going off or a frog falling into my lap. I would get so mad. But, well, I wouldn't stay mad, couldn't stay mad at you. You would pout your cute little pout, and then all would be forgiven."

"God," Stanley cries to his surrounding family, "I love you all!"

The river flows. Whether it be time or aging or life-giving water, the river flows.

"Our small town was situated on a clean and cool river where we swam all summer long, the whole of our population, all one thousand one-hundred and seventy-eight of us. Even ninety-three-year-old Ethel Jenkins, born in our town and destined to die there, took a dip now and then wearing a bathing suit she must have worn fifty years before. But…"

"Anything less would be immodest!"

"'Anything less would be immodest,' she would say."

S and T and now even R are enraptured by Stanley's beatific portrait of his childhood home and life. Were that they had had…

"The river was the center of all social activity. We held picnics at the river, and dances, and the county fair. We met our first sweethearts there. Got our first kisses there. Maybe even first experienced the darker side of love there. And some drowned there, almost, it seemed, as unintentional sacrifices to appease this mother of us all. This summer—this summer that I am talking about—this summer of the '55 Caddy, and Mom trying to teach little Billy Ackerman to play chopsticks, and of my sister's coming of age—this summer is dear to me for the growth I achieved and the revelations I received as I crossed that danger fraught line between childhood and adolescence."

Stanley stops with such a pleasant smile on his aged, gray face that he looks almost cute, almost boy-like, almost attractive.

"Well, Mr. Lewis," S says, wondering how to bottle up what she felt so that she could take it home, "an enviable childhood, indeed. Now, let me ask you about—

"All this last bit," Stanley slowly says, his smile slowly becoming less bucolic and more bubonic, "was bullshit."

"I'm sorry," S says in confusion. "What do you mean by 'bullshit'?"

Stanley looks at S, amused at her dimness. "Bullshit," Stanley repeats as if repetition will explain. "You know— horse pucky; crap; false; phony; fabricated; made-up—a lie! But I've always wanted to do that. Tell a story so kind and warm and saturated with nostalgia that I could package it up neat to sell it to all you suckers."

"Now, Mr. Lewis," T says, S having been stung into silence, "we really need the truth—

"Or, or something like what TV reporters were always doing. You know, taking you back to some Roots of America place, some 'real' America place where things were 'simple' and 'easy-going.' You know, 'Mainstream America.' Gave you comfort to know that it really did exist. Actually, it wouldn't have mattered where I took you. It's a state of mind, isn't it? I mean, I could have given you some big city nostalgia, telling you about living in romantic and mystic buildings called brownstones or walk-ups. I could have told you of kind-hearted supers with thick accents who represented the best of immigrant America. I could have told you about the heat of a city summer and cooling off in a gushing fire hydrant, and that would have charmed your little hearts as much as any old fucking river! Or I could have given you a farm fantasy, a remembrance of childhood close to the soil, where I was instilled with the value of hard work for an honest dollar, and where the face of God was revealed to me in the birth of a calf."

Stanley looks suddenly and directly at R, a bully bested. "You would have liked that, wouldn't you?"

R, who has been trying to get a word in edgewise, lets out his built-up frustration and impatience in a long sigh articulating, "No, Mr. Lewis, I would *not* have liked that."

"What? Not have liked to be moved by my stories of family life, love, and struggles in hayseed America? For God's sake, why not?"

"Because they would not have been true," R states the fact.

"True? Shit! They're never true. They're just little comforts holding up values you want to believe in despite what day-to-day experience tells you. But I'm sorry; I have no comforts to give."

"We are not asking—

"And I cannot make you feel good. Why should I? You want that crap—watch TV! For I didn't grow up in no Goddamn nostalgic small town; I didn't grow up in no two-story clapboard crap house on a tree-shaded shit street! I didn't grow up among neighbors who were songs; I didn't have a river; my dad didn't buy a Caddy, and my mom could not play the piano! So what? I HAD THE MOON!"

Stanley looks up and gestures to a full moon brilliantly bouncing off sunlight, stunning in its stark beauty, and unseen, of course, by R and S and T.

Even if it had been there, R would not have seen it as he had closed his eyes just as Stanley had opened his heart; and had hoped for a quick cessation—or maybe an early death. "Are—you—finished?" R asks with a toxic spray that shrinks Stanley.

"I'm sorry," Stanley says weakly.

"Sorry for what?"

"Sorry for whatever the tone in your voice is accusing me of having done."

R feels he finally has Stanley on the hook, and he's not going to let him off. "*We* came up here at great expense. *You* said you would cooperate."

"You ask questions; I answer."

"No! You admit it yourself—you make up answers. Why?"

"It's fun."

"Is this an occasion for fun?"

"I'll take any occasion I can get," Stanley says, almost too quietly to hear.

Sad case, sad case, R was damn tired of having to draw from sad cases. Still, best now to show some sympathy, manufactured though it might be. "Look, Mr. Lewis, I know your life is not perfect."

"My life is just fine. Thank you very much. Go fuck yourself!"

R suppresses a scream and turns to S and T. "This is useless! *He* is useless. He will not speak the truth—

"You want the truth? The big 'why?'"

"Yes, Mr. Lewis," S, who has remained calm and not a little amused over R's frustration, uses her calm to what she hopes will be a good effect. "Yes, Mr. Lewis, please."

"I can't imagine it being of interest to you."

The thought intrigues T. "Why do you say that?"

"I tried to tell you about the moon—

"We do not want justifications!" R yells the point straight at Stanley.

S, almost motherly, places a hand on R's arm. "We just want the simple, plain truth, Mr. Lewis, that's all." Like an adolescent son, R is repulsed by S's hand and slides his arm out from under it.

"If I cannot talk about the moon—

"What the hell does the moon have to do with anything?" R shouts again.

"That's what I've been trying to tell—

"Are you trying to tell us the moon had some sort of strange astrological-gravitational pull on your actions?"

"Of course not. That's absurd."

"Well then," R's anger is now coming through clenched teeth. "Keep it simple. Where did you really grow up?"

Filtered through R's teeth, the anger is sharp and stinging, like nettles beating a young child. And a young child Stanley now becomes, scared of being chastised, chastised into fear. "A suburb." He says meekly. "That's where I really grew up. A suburb in Southern California on the western edge of the continent with nowhere to go but the Pacific Ocean—and I could not swim."

R and T, long-time swimmers themselves, are incredulous. Stanley can see that. It is as plain as a poke in the chest. "Sure. Yeah. There were people who grew up in Southern California who never learned to swim. We were all given lessons, of course, that came with the sunshine. I had my lesson at the age of five. My instructor was from the sink or swim school."

The city plunge, all hard and chlorine-wet pavement, and tiles, cracked here and there, senseless sounds reverberating off walls and ground, causing confusion; sunshine reflecting off clear water stinging eyes with dancing glints. It is enormous, an ocean in miniature, foreboding despite its cheerful blue bottom distorted by the water, and the water singing a splashing siren's song offering an inviting shift of reality.

"Stanley Lewis?" The swim instructor yells out to the five-year-old, butt on pavement, back against the wall of the changing rooms of

slapping feet echoing and showers streaming. "Okay, Stanley, your turn."

"I don't want to," small-for-his-age, skinny little slip of humanity Stanley squeaks out, fear choking more than just his throat.

"Now, Stanley, all the other kids have jumped in."

"I'm scared."

"There's nothing to be scared of. It's just water."

Stanley does not budge, and the swim instructor is forced to go to Stanley and offer him a hand up.

"No!"

The swim instructor grabs Stanley by his upper right arm, "Come on, Stanley, in we go," and swings him up and carries him like a sack to the pool.

"No, no, no!"

The swim instructor gets a good grip on Stanley, lifts him a little, then sends him off, up briefly into the air, then down as gravity will have it, to meet his wet, undulating fate.

"I plunged! Deeper and deeper and deeper. I didn't think I was ever going to stop. I didn't think I was ever going to come up," Stanley draws in a deep breath and freezes while he holds it. R and S and T watch, curious at how much Stanley makes memory physical. They notice he seems to be turning blue. Concern is considered, but finally, Stanley blows out his held breath. "But I did—gagging and screaming and crying; flailing and kicking, not knowing if I would ever be able to grasp, to hold on, to feel something solid ever again!"

The swim instructor reaches down with his extended right arm and grabs Stanley under his left underarm, and yanks him up and out of the pool to set him standing and dripping on his two little feet, his body shivering, his teeth chattering, his breath rushing in and out. "Stanley, you're not supposed to sink. You're supposed to swim. Do you understand that? Swim, not sink! Do you think you can get it right this time?" He grabs Stanley for another toss, but Stanley stiffens and falls to his knees and grabs the aqua-man around his legs, and refuses to let go. The swim instructor is disgusted at the display and gives up. "Oh, okay, baby. Go get dressed."

"I didn't continue with the lessons. I begged my mother not to send me back. She didn't. I never learned how to swim, just sort of dog paddle. I could keep my head above water—but with no grace."

R, with impatience, S with sympathy, T with a slight disdain, sit silently, waiting for Stanley to continue.

"Oh, well, anyway—the suburb I lived in, it was brand new when we moved in. It had been an orange grove just before we got there. They were all pulled up in 1951 to make room to build these little, square blocks colored, like with crayons, in bumpy stucco and laid out, one after the other, in two alternating styles for diversity—bing, bang, bing, bang, bing—to create lower middle class or upper lower class—take your pick—Southern California suburban neighborhoods.

"The sun shone harshly on such neighborhoods, for nothing stood in its way. No multistory buildings. No ancestral trees. My family moved into our house when I was only three and a half. But I can remember the landscape clearly. The houses were naked, with no owner-applied dressings yet, like awnings or flower boxes or trim painted another color than the original. Or a front porch expanded and extended. The yards were dusty brown waiting for seed and water. The sidewalks were so newly white they reflected the harsh sunlight directly into your eyes. And the streets were so fresh with black asphalt they were spongy and seemed in mid-melt under the sun.

"In time, all this changed. The bing-bang houses took on individual attributes. The yards became covered with grass and the shade of young trees. The sidewalks cracked and darkened; the streets cracked and faded.

"But the essential fact of this Southern California suburban neighborhood never changed. It was a place people came to, or a place people left—but it was never a place people came from.

"So, this is where I grew up. My house was a bing house. And the lawn in front of it was the lawn where I laid as the moon made… Well, the spot where I discovered the moon. And two houses down was a bang house—bang houses were better than bing houses, everybody knew that. They were upscale models; they had an extra bedroom and a family room—anyway, in that bang house is where I discovered space. I mean, not just space, you know, the concept of nothing between two somethings, but space, Outer Space. Black. Weightless. Starry. In its way, solid, as solid and real as the moon. I mean, like an ocean. But—but everywhere, not just in some pit on a planet.

"How did I discover space? Through every child's great guru gadget, of course."

The two acolytes to the flicker prostrate themselves before the 25-inch RCA television in the mahogany Pensbury cabinet resting on curved but skinny legs, which Stanley finds fascinating—can they really hold the weight? He reaches out to touch the slender, mahogany-shiny limbs.

"Don't touch, Stan, just look!"

"In that bang house lived my best boyhood friend, Hank. Hank was a snot."

"Don't eat ice cream over the carpet! Stay in the kitchen!"

"He would tell me in ritual language handed down from his parents. He ate ice cream over the carpet, of course, providing his mother wasn't there, but that was okay, it was his house, and anyway...."

"You're always messing things up, Stan, so be careful."

Chastisement. Comes from without, nestles within. Stanley feels it like undigested shame.

"Anyway, this is where I discovered Outer Space. It was on a kid's show called *Marshall Bob*, which we watched at lunchtime while eating baloney sandwiches on white bread with butter. Marshall Bob was this tall guy with a big, broad grin who seemed to like us. He sang songs, taught us how to brush our teeth, and had special guests, like policemen who told us not to be scared of policemen. And a dog pound guy who told us not to be mean to our pets."

"How tall do you think Marshall Bob is," Hank asks Stanley, a mashed bit of white bead stuck in the gap between his two upper front

teeth.

"Don't know."

"Betcha he's as tall as my dad. My dad's real tall. You're dad's short."

"He is not!"

"Is too. He's real short. Means you're going to be real short. I'm going to be tall, like my dad."

"So?"

"So?"

"So what?"

"So you'll see."

"And Marshall Bob ran cartoons! Which is what we were really there for. We really liked all those funny animals running around hitting each other and blowing things up—Ha!" Stanley stops and points to R and S and T, all scratching their facility-issued pens across recycled paper. "Boy, I can imagine your reaction to that last bit. You're all making quick notes, aren't you? Oooh! Lewis said something significant! Betcha you're theorizing already. Well, whatever your theory is—give it up."

S and T follow R's lead and say nothing after they finish their notes. By their silence, they encourage Stanley to end his.

"It's coming on! It" coming on!"

Hank from long ago grabs Stanley's attention, making him see the beginning of another cartoon.

"One of the cartoons was different. It was serious. It was about Space Spirit, a good guy in a rocketship in the

27th century who flew through space fighting, you know, bad guys. It was his rocket ship that intrigued me. Wow! Now I knew how to get into Outer Space. And through Outer Space to the moon!"

"Well, son, there really aren't such things," Stanley's mother, having coffee with Hank's mother, says. "It's all made up. You can't go into space, Stanley. It's impossible. You can't go to the moon."

Stanley closes his eyes as if somehow that would also close his ears—or his mind.

When he opens them again, he finds R and S and T, their eyes open, if not their minds. He asks them, "Have you ever had that problem?"

"What problem?" S wants to know.

"Getting opinions you never asked for."

"Oh, I always ask for opinions."

"No kidding?"

"It's part of my job."

"But even though you asked for them—do you really like getting opinions?"

"Well…"

"A-ha! Ask and ye shall receive. But the real problem is not asking and still receiving. I never asked my mother's opinion as to whether I could or could not go to the moon. I didn't need to. I always knew I would. I didn't know how. I just always figured it would happen. So I didn't ask. I just made a statement: I'm going to the moon someday!"

"I'm going to the moon someday," Stanley says as he lays on a blanket on the front lawn in front of his gathered-in-lawn-chairs fam-

ily—mom, dad, sister. He stares up at the moon halfway in waning or waxing, but, in either case, bright as a lamp, even the dark half just tissue-thin visible, which, oddly, makes the whole moon seem solid, hard, and round. Mom sits with her legs crossed at her ankles and smokes her Parliament cigarette; dad sits with his feet firmly planted on the ground and drinks his can of Lucky Lager beer; sister sits in a pool of boredom because all the TV shows are in reruns.

"You can't go to the moon, Stanley. It's impossible," his mother says. "Who would want to go to the moon anyway? There's no trees up there."

"I'm going to the moon someday."

"Well, son, you never know." Says his father, a universally nice man, "Maybe in your lifetime they'll figure out a way to get up there, but certainly not in mine."

"Why would anyone want to go up there anyway? There's no trees!" His mom says again, with emphasis, in case they had not appreciated the cleverness of her statement the first time.

"I'm going to the moon someday!"

"That's stupid!" His sister declares from her pool of boredom.

"Did I have to believe them?" Stanley asks S sincerely. He really wants to know. "I thought for a while that I had to. I mean, this was my mother whose tummy I would lay on to hear it gurgle. And this was my father who fixed everything and told me everything would be okay when I threw up. My sister? Who the hell ever believes sisters? But parents? How could I not believe my parents?"

S has no answer and makes that clear by raising her eyebrows.

But it doesn't matter because Stanley has the answer. "Easy. I knew the moon. I knew its friendship. I knew space. I knew it was there. I knew that men had conjured up spaceships. I knew of their existence in films, little dreams of seeming reality. Why would it not all come together in big realities steaming with drama?

"To counteract the dreariness of parent-speak, I turned to what all kids turn to, play, physical dream-making. I made my bedroom the cabin of a spaceship; my window the porthole; the view out of that porthole all of space, and my pajamas, a spacesuit! Not bulky and protective like real spacesuits, but neat and colorful with an emblem on the chest, like Space Spirit's, because that was the only thing I knew. But unlike Space Spirit, I didn't go to a bunch of unpronounceable planets to ferret out evil—I just went to the moon!"

Stanley sits in his cockpit-bed, making final checks until it is time to go.

"*10—9—8—7654321, BLAST OFF!*

"*Clearing Earth's air!*

"*Set course for the moon!*

"*Prepare for landing!*

"*Turn ship tail down!*

"*Touchdown!*"

"And then I would step out onto the moon. But first, I had to get past my parents in the living room. Then I would go into the kitchen, to the back door, and quietly open it and step into the night-dark backyard and explore...stepping slowly across the surface of the moon...seeing the stars above, bright spots in my life...trying to know the quiet I assumed would be there."

"Stanley! What are you doing out there?"

"Parent-reality would intrude."

"Uh, looking for Stubby, Mom!"

"Stubby, the cat."

"Stubby's inside asleep on the couch! Now get in here!"

"I come in and collect the cat—as if I really want Stubby to sleep with me—which makes me cute in the eyes of my parents—and take him into my bedroom and put him on the bed: a moon creature I have found and adopted! I climb into the cockpit. I check the instruments, start the engines, radio to Earth, strap myself in, hit the switch, and —"

"Blast off!"

"Mom! Stanley's talking to himself again!"

"Stanley! Shut up and go to sleep!"

"Things changed a lot in 1957 when I was eight years old."

It is a warm summer night. Dad comes out of their small bing house and crosses the front lawn, heading for two lawn chairs, followed by Mom and Sister. Dad points up high into the sky. "There it is!"

"The Russians put this ball on the end of a rocket and launched it into Earth orbit, the first man-made object in Earth orbit, the first man-created thing in space. On one day, 'sputnik' was just a funny, meaningless Russian word. On the next day, it had a meaning so deep that few could define it."

"*There it is!*" *Dad says.*

"*Where? Where?*" *Mom asks.*

"*There! See it? Like a star moving.*" *Dad guides.*

"*It's going to drop bombs on us!*" *Sister yells, drops, and covers.*

No, it's not, honey," *Dad reassures.* "*It's up too high.*"

But sister is not assured and continues to fetal on the lawn, burying her head in her arms as her parents continue the conversation

"*How high up is it?*"

"*Well, I don't know exactly. But it's really up there.*"

"*Did you see what it looked like in the paper? It's just this ball thing.*"

"*Well, yeah, but it's got things inside.*"

"*I don't understand why they put it up there.*"

"*Just to show they could do it, I guess.*"

"*But why? What's the use?*"

"*Well, I guess they guess they got one.*"

"*Well, I don't see it. There's nothing up there but empty space.*"

Stanley had already been outside. Laying flat on his back on his blanket in front of the lawn chairs—as low as he could go. But he was high with awe and wonder. "*I'm going up there someday!*"

"*You can't go up there, Stanley. It's impossible. They may be able to send little balls up there, but they can't send people. Who would want to go up there, anyway?*"

"*I'm going up there someday!*"

"*Well, son, you never know. Maybe in your lifetime they'll figure out how to put a man up there. But certainly not in mine.*"

"*But it's nothing but empty space up there!*"

"I'm going up there someday!"

Risking armageddon, sister rises up and out from under her arms to draw from her font of wisdom and declare, "That's stupid!"

Stanley stands as if propelled by a rocket, and steps towards R and S and T, causing a flash of concern, allayed when Stanley stops and addresses the three of them as if they were a hall of humanity.

"I'll tell you how stupid it was. One month later, the Russians put up Sputnik 2 with a payload of over one thousand pounds, including a live dog! A live, living, breathing Earth creature! In January of '58, America sent up its first satellite, Vanguard 1. And then, in July, NASA was formed. And then, in February of '59, NASA established a working group on lunar exploration! And then on May 25th, 1961—MY BIRTHDAY!—On May 25th, 1961, President Kennedy told us that we should commit ourselves to reaching and landing on the moon by the end of the decade. That's how stupid it was! Kennedy! Not some old fart president with no hair, with a frail or bulky body, but Kennedy! Young, tall, 20th century to his teeth, 21st century in his vision. Handsome! The future seemed handsome!"

"Well, I'll tell ya, I never thought they would do it in my lifetime."

"Why would anyone want to go to the moon? There's no trees."

"It's stupid!"

"Mr. Lewis, sit back down," R says.

"What?"

"Take your chair again, Mr. Lewis."

"Why?"

"We want you to be comfortable," S suggests with a smile.

"You are not allowed to invade our space," T tells him

"Your space?"

"That's right."

"Oh!" Stanley leaps back. "Sorry, sorry." He sits back down in his chair and waits, as he often had, for whatever would be next.

R, happy they can now continue, says, "Now, Mr. Lewis, this obsession with the moon—

"What obsession?"

"Well, Mr. Lewis, that's all you seem to want to talk about," S says very kindly.

"That makes it an obsession?"

"By strict definition, I would certainly think so."

"What would you call it if you shared it?"

S has no answer, but T does. "Mr. Lewis, you're the one who wants to talk about it, not us."

"Yes, I've noticed."

"But as it does seem important to you," R grabs control again, hopefully of the whole situation, "let me ask this: You say as a child, even as an infant, you wanted to go to the moon. But, of course, at that time, no one was going to the moon. It was hardly a realistic desire. Then things changed. The impossible had become possible. Fantasy had become a reality. Did you now begin to prepare? To enter into a course of rigorous study that would prepare you to become an astronaut, for example?"

"Well…"

"Yes?"

"Well…"

"Yes?"

"Um…"

"The clock ticks, Mr. Lewis. Time moves forward, and I am aging rapidly," S says sternly.

"I read books."

"Books? What kind of books?"

"I started with those of facts."

"Books on space? Astrophysics? Science in general?"

"Yeah. Some like that."

"And…?"

"And I found the facts hard going. I would get half a page—I would fall asleep."

"And so?"

"And so I turned to fiction. That was nice. Everything was there. The whole spectrum of possibilities."

"*Science* fiction?" R sneers, masquerading a statement as a question.

"Sci-fi, I think it also used to be called," S gently says.

"SF, I've also heard it called," T adds to be helpful.

"Yes," Stanley says. "All those."

"And where did that lead you?" R asks.

"Well, by the time I was, oh, fourteen or so, I had decided my future would be as a space taxi driver."

T snorts, somewhat unbecomingly. "A space taxi driver?

That's absurd."

"No, it's not!"

"A space taxi driver is stupid!" His sister says as she sits in a chair in the living room during a commercial break from American Bandstand.

"No, it's not!"

"There's no such thing."

"But there's going to be."

"There is not! You're the stupidest brother!"

"And you're the dumbest sister!"

Mom is lying on the couch reading her LIFE magazine, letting the siblings spar, assuming—wrongly—that they will eventually outgrow such contention.

"Well, I don't say there are taxis in space."

"I didn't say, now!"

"Why would you want to be anything so stupid?"

"Because."

"Because why?"

"Because!"

"Yeah, but because why?"

"JUST BECAUSE!"

"Stannnley!" Mom, in her sly way, breaks up the fight by intruding. "You ought to read what it says here. The training those astronauts have to go through! Hard to imagine. And what they have to know to even become astronauts! And you ought to see, come here, you should see this picture of the inside of their spaceship. Look at all those instruments! How do they ever figure out what button to push?"

"You see," Stanley pleads his case to R and S and T, "I

figured the space taxi would be small and easy to handle and have about as many dials and buttons as my dad's car. And I would get a route from here to the moon and back, so I would get to go to the moon a lot, traveling through the space in-between. And there would be this bubble dome top so I could see all of space around me. I would also be independent, as I assumed all taxi drivers were, answering to no one. At least they seemed so in the movies. I would have fun, I figured, in my little yellow bubble-domed space taxi going to the moon and back."

"THAT'S STUPID!"

Stanley cringes for no perceivable—to R and S and T—reason.

"Yes—stupid. But—but you have to understand, to me, at that time, a time so near the first real moon landing, yet when the idea was still being denigrated as *science fiction*. A time when I was very young, yet filled with ancient desires, and when my mind gave me no aid with well-thought-out words to explain my feelings. Anything, *anything* that seemed a way to the moon, was anything but stupid. It was, in fact—sublime. If I could not be an astronaut—and my mom seemed to believe that I could not—then I would be a space taxi driver. It was simple logic to my young mind that gave me simple assurances."

+

Marc Starr, Space Hack

by Stanley Lewis

It was a day just like any other day on the Goddard Space Wheel orbiting three hundred miles above the surface of the planet: it was nice. When you live in a controlled environment there isn't much variation in weather. The temperature is always perfect, the airflow is optimal, the ambient light is bright enough to see with no glare to confuse. If you have some misguided desire to experience weather patterns, well you can always go to one of the huge observation windows, as most of our residents do, to look down on the Earth with intoxicated-like awe and wonder at the creeping clouds below. Me? Whenever I pass any of these windows, I just look down on the Earth—period.

Yeah, a day just like any other day. Except it was the day she came into my life.

I'm Marc Starr, space hack. I have the Goddard to Luna run, and I like it. I spend my days and artificial nights ferrying back and forth Homo sapiens, most of whom hardly deserve the appellation. Or, maybe the problem is that they do.

I was standing in my taxi stall, minding my own business, which I'm very good at doing, polishing my little yellow bubble-domed space taxi, enjoying a moment's peace when that peace was broken.

"Taxi!"

He was a businessman, some exploiter of the moon, you could tell that by his suit, dark and serious hiding something darker. Or maybe he was a politician, a manipulator of the moon, trying to bring it down-to-earth with his "policies." Or maybe he was just a bureaucrat, a crude little toady to either the businessman or the politician. It really doesn't matter--at first sight I loathed him.

"Yes, that's what it is all right," I admitted to the fact while still polishing.

"Well? Are you on duty or not?"

"I don't know. Depends where you want to go." I loved the little waves of incredulity that passed over his face.

"Why to the moon, of course."

"Yeah? Why?"

"I've got my reasons."

"Yeah? Well, there's a million reasons why a man might want to go to the moon. Most of them adulterated. And I think most of the adulterators have helped buff the shine on my cab's back seat. But, hey, I don't hold it against them. I never turn down a fare and I rarely refuse a request. You want to go for an unauthorized orbit? Fine by me. You in a hurry and want to push the speed a little? Okay. Just hang onto your hat. Or you want a nice slow ride so you can get in some zero g nookie in the back seat with some space station slut? No problem. I won't even look. And I'll ignore the sounds. Want a quick flyby over your competitor's mines? Why not? I've got this law, you see, the law of the gentleman space hack I like to call it. To wit: the Homo sapien in the back pays the fare, the Homo sapien in the back calls the shots."

"Good. Then let's go."

"But I got my preferences." I stopped him from entering my hack by a poke of my finger on his puffed-up chest. "And my preferences run to fares who just sit down, shut up, and stare at space. That's why I got off ol' shaky terra firma in the first place—for the vast, quiet, diamond-studded vacuum of space, where a man can think, be himself, and die without causing a ruckus."

"Okay. Got it. Let's go."

The slithering, slick sapien tried to de-poke himself from my finger, but I would not have it. "Of course, every once in a while I got to put up with fares who don't sit down and shut up. The ones who yak for the sake of yakking, or out of some misguided notion that I desire their company. But, like I say, they pays the fare, they calls the shots. They want to talk--I talk with them. That's how I know most of them ain't worth brushing asteroid dust off of."

"Okay, I won't say a word."

He moved to get in; I moved to keep him out. "You'd be surprised what people tell a space hack they wouldn't tell their own best friend. The funny thing is, they always tell me to 'Keep it to yourself'. So who am I going to tell?"

"Taxi!"

It was a woman who perfectly belonged in space--for she was heavenly. She had an hourglass figure that you wanted to run your sands of time through. Legs that ascended from earth to heaven and which you wanted to hold in good standing. Breasts that made their points with full and firm logic and allowed for no rebuttal. And it was all wrapped in a red space jumper that made you want to jump her. And she had a face that spoke volumes--and they were all dirty stories.

"Beat it, buddy," I said to my former fare.

"Hey! I was here first."

"Right. And now you're the first to leave. Get lost."

Miffed and disgruntled, Mr. Dark Suit stomped away as Walks-in-Beauty glided up to me.

"Lunar base?" I politely inquired.

"Yes, please," she said in a voice that gave new meaning to the term, 'Music of the Spheres'."

With the most gentle of touches I guided her into the back seat of my little yellow bubble-domed space taxi, then slipped into the driver's seat up front.

"But, uh, I'm in no hurry," she said, double entendre-ing to beat the band. Or something like that.

"Yeah, being in a hurry is no good. Getting there early sometimes spoils the fun."

"I hate spoiled fun."

"Yeah. I don't blame ya."

I started the engines on my little yellow bubble-domed space taxi, then blasted off. Soon we were in space, in a universe of possibilities. She had nothing to say at first. And I had nothing to say that was appropriate. Then she leaned forward in her seat, close to the back of my neck, and warmed it with her sweet breath as she said, "You're Marc Starr, aren't you?"

"That's what it says on my hack's license."

"I mean, the Marc Starr."

"Well, I don't know of any other."

"I've heard a lot about you, Mr. Starr."

"Yeah? Well, I take credit for the good and deny the bad."

"Everything I've heard is good--especially about the bad."

I could tell we shared deep, empathic feelings. I couldn't help but wonder if this was going to be a match made in deep space-- if only I could make her in deep space.

"They say you're the best space hack pilot that's ever been."

"Is that what they say?"

"Yeah, that's what they say. They also say that even though all you drive is this little yellow bubble-domed space taxi, you're a better pilot than ninety-nine percent of the space jocks in the Space Service."

"Is that what they say?"

"Yeah, that's what they say. They say you really know your way around the spaceways."

"Is that really what they say?"

"Yeah, that's really what they say."

"Well, I'm never one to argue with the crowd."

"It's a man like you who could make a woman like me very, very happy."

"Do they say that also?"

"No, that's my personal opinion."

"Yeah? Well, how'd you like to dart behind a satellite in the satellite graveyard and turn your soft opinion into hard knowledge?"

"No."

"No!?"

"No. I don't like doing it in zero g. Not

enough—friction."

"Oh."

"I like it in the low g of the moon. The moon was made for love, you know."

"Yeah? I always wondered what that old man was smiling about."

"When we get to the moon, you can come up to my place—come as often as you would like."

"'Like' ain't the word, lady."

"If..."

"Oh-oh."

"If you're wearing your uniform."

"My what?"

"You're uniform. That of a captain in the Space Service. I _love_ a man in uniform."

"Well, that's damn silly, seeing how all you want to do is get him out of it!"

"It's important to set the proper romantic mood."

That was it. I cut the propulsions and fired the retros and stopped dead in space. Then I turned around to face the face trying to launch my thousand ships. "Listen, lady, what's your name? Uncle Sam?"

As she smiled, she very slowly blinked her

eyes. "No. It's Galaxina, Andromeda Galaxina."

"Oh, now I get it! <u>Major</u> Andromeda Galaxina, I believe it is. The Space Service's special officer for recruitment and, at times, I presume, shanghai?"

"That's right Mr. Starr. And I want you!"

"Yeah, like I said—Uncle Sam."

"Did Uncle Sam ever have a pair of these?"

With swift grace and a wicked smile, the Major parted the red sea of the front of her jumper and let loose two large, firm, golden-skin orbs that called out to all of <u>Man</u>kind to orbit, land, and plant the flag of conquest.

"Hey, lady, put them back!"

Genuine perplexity mapped itself on her face. "You don't like them?"

"Not when they're pointing the way to the recruitment office!"

Somewhat chagrined, the Major closed and secured her bulkhead.

"Boy, lady, sending you to me, that's—well, that's a real black hole."

"Pardon?"

"I mean it sucks, lady!"

"We want you, Mr. Starr. We want you real bad."

"Yeah, I know. But I'll tell you what I've told everybody else: I'm not a joiner. I don't like being part of a group. You understand? I like the stars, space, the moon, and the quiet and the freedom to enjoy them. I rent my services out, bit by bit, now and then. But I won't sell them to anyone. Not for money, not for glory, and not for nookie, zero g or low g, it don't matter. You got all that down in your beautiful little head?"

"Unhappily so."

"Well, good. So tell your generals that, and tell them for me to take a great big leap into the great big dipper! Okay?"

"They're not going to be happy."

"What am I, Little Jimmy Sunshine I gotta make people happy? Look, Lady, blame yourself--for you've broken the code of space."

"And just what is that?"

"Let a man be, lady, let a man be..."

+

"Mr. Lewis?" S calls for Stanley's attention. When she

gets it, she asks, "When did you first start thinking about sex, Mr. Lewis?"

"I don't want to talk about that," Stanley says, squirming slightly as if his chair had become not only uncomfortable but irritating.

"Well, Mr. Lewis, it might be interesting to—

"It might be interesting for you, but what do I get out of it?"

"Well, sex plays a big part in most people's lives."

"Yeah?"

"Yes."

"Then I'm sure you have enough to handle. Next subject?"

Sensing an open, possibly festering, sore, R decides a little salt is just the seasoning required. "Most people start dealing with sexual feelings in their adolescence."

"Oh, yeah," Stanley says as if reminded of something. "Adolescence. Too old to cry; too young to die. Eyes too big from looking; hands too small for touching. I hated adolescence!"

"Oh, there must have been," T joined in, "something about that time you remember fondly."

"Well..." A warm, colorful glow comes over Stanley.

"Yes?"

"Comic book superheroes."

"Yes, of course!" T gets it. "The myth creatures of the 20th Century. Did you have a favorite?"

"I had several." Some old glee graces Stanley's face.

R, not liking comic book superheroes as much as sex, but knowing that the tide goes where it must, decides to go along. "Why did you like comic book superheroes?"

Stanley does not answer. Stanley is seeing the colorful fly and punch and stretch and burst into flames and speed faster than sound and become invisible and change from this and that to that and this and back again.

With patience leaking from his pores, R pushes, "Mr. Lewis?"

Nothing.

R pokes, "Mr. Lewis?"

More nothing—if there can be more of nothing.

R prods. "Mr. Lewis!" Sharply. "MR. LEWIS!"

"Hey, Lewis! Short stuff! Booger eater! Give me that comic book!"

A sharp prod strikes and sticks in Stanley's sternum, causing not pain but the fear of pain. But still, the precious must be held onto. 'Uh, no. It's—it's mine."

"Hey, I'm not asking," the schoolyard, after-school, even weekend bully shouts, "I'm telling! Give me that comic book or I'm going to beat the crap out of you!"

Stanley collapses and quivers, and everything shakes but his resolve. "It's—it's mine."

"Alright, you asked for it!"

The bully snatches the comic book out of Stanley's clutching hand, ripping the cover, and throws it into the mud, and stomps on it. He turns to Stanley and stomps on him, on his stomach, stomps again, then lands a blow on Stanley's head, then kicks him in his chest, once, twice, a third time to make a point; ribs crack, one breaks. The bully places his big foot on Stanley's head and pushes down, grinding it into the ground. He stops and stands back to appreciate his handiwork. It's good, he's pleased, but he's not done yet. He grabs one of Stanley's hands, pulls it up, and breaks his little finger, then pulls Stanley's arms behind his back and forces them to move in directions nature never intended. Finally, inspired by adrenalin, he pinches Stanley's nostrils, grabs the muddy comic book, and shoves it into Stanley's open, breathing mouth. Then the bully laughs and laughs and laughs and walks away, pleased as the punches he has given broken, bloody Stanley.

Stanley groans and groans and groans...

Stanley slumps in his chair, groaning with the weight of the memory. S assumes Stanley's pain is being lived and felt again, and S has some little compassion for him. "Mr. Lewis," she says gently, "how badly were you hurt?"

Stanley struggles through the pain, "Wha—what do you mean?"

"When this bully beat you up—how badly were you hurt?"

Stanley swiftly sits up, straight and calm and unperturbed. "Oh, that? Never really happened."

R is pissed. "Mr. Lewis, it—

"I was only shoved around now and them—

"Mr. Lewis, it would really be helpful if—

"But such a beating is what I was always afraid of."

"It would really be helpful if you could stick to the facts!"

"I thought you wanted the truth."

"Facts are truth!"

"That's not what she said," Stanley points to T.

"What?" R is confused.

T is not. "Uh, yeah, I said something about facts being in the file, and truth being—

"Oh, yes. You do have a way with words." R addresses T, showing no appreciation for her way with words. "Mr. Lewis, let me put it this way. I'm asking you to document your life, not fictionalize it. That's all. Please."

"I could go, you know," Stanley says.

"Yes, that's right."

"Nothing's keeping me here."

"True."

"True, hell, it's a fact!"

"But you want to tell us, don't you, Mr. Lewis?" The perceptive T says. "You need to tell us."

"Do you think this is a confession?"

"No. But I would like it to be a revelation."

A revelation? To reveal and to have that revelation heard. The idea moves Stanley powerfully, and the movement tells on his face.

S sees the opening. "Now, besides living in fear of bullies, how did you spend your time in high school?"

"I spent a lot of it on the athletic field."

R and S and T each look at the little thin man before them and have to wonder. It is not a hidden wonder.

"Surprises you, doesn't it? What the hell was the fucking little wimp, shrimp doing on the athletic field?" Stanley turns his eyes to R. "You just asked yourself that, didn't you?"

"No, Mr. Lewis." R defends himself. "I did not."

"Come on, admit it, didn't you?"

"Let's continue, shall we?"

"I know you didn't mean to. It was just a reflex of the brain. You're really a fair person, right? But boy, it would fry your ass pretty good if I told you I was one of the swiftest, deadliest fielders my high school had ever seen. Or that I was the most accurate field goal kicker ever in high school football. It wouldn't fit in with your conception of truth, would it? Well, don't sweat it. I was none of those things. What I was doing out on the athletic field had nothing to do with athletics."

"So," S asks, "what *were* you doing on the athletic field?"

"It should be obvious...."

But it isn't. Not to R or S or T.

"You don't get it?"

"Please, Mr. Lewis, if—

"It was a much bigger lawn than my own! Big and—and open to the sky. Trees eventually did grow in my suburb. Fucking green foliage obscuring the view! But here—here I had the vast sky open to me. No obstructions between me and my moon."

Stanley stands and seems to be somewhere else. He walks around the room and narrates in mime what he describes in words. "I would sneak out of the house late at night, taking my dad's binoculars and a lawn chair. I would then walk to the high school, which was just down the street. I would climb the fence—my only athletic ability—go to the middle of the field, set down my lawn chair, sit in it, raise the binoculars to my eyes—and commune. Commune until the moon dipped below the horizon."

He ends back in his chair, and looking at R and S and T through his pair of thumb-and-forefingers binoculars, says, "Sometimes, while sitting there, I would have fantasies. Wonderful fantasies. Fantasies of easy ways of leaving the Earth."

It is a quiet night. Most traffic is home asleep. Dogs are choosing not to bark. There is no wind, not even a breeze. The stillness is comfortable.

The moon is full and brilliantly white and high in the sky. Stanley leans back and props his neck on the back of the lawn chair to steady his head as he looks through the binoculars and "travels" to the moon to see the craters and mountains and mare. They all seem so real and solid that he feels he can touch them and wants to cry when his grasp reaches out and finds nothing but the windless air.

The bright white of the moon and the deep black of the sky are suddenly curtained by colors. Red, green, yellow, blue; red, green, yellow, blue—coming, streaming, flashing, swishing, announcing the landing of a spacecraft of no known human design. Stanley is scared. Stanley is fascinated. Stanley is apprehensive. Stanley is drawn. Then Stanley is bathed in one pure white beam of light.

A voice fills his head with words. A voice not human; words not English. And yet Stanley is comfortable with them. And Stanley understands them.

"Yes. Yes, Zolnixitrude, you are quite correct. He is the perfect one. Such a pure being. Such unadulterated sincerity. Such essential truth."

A sound both mechanical and biological sings to Stanley as a door in the craft opens, and a long ramp, like a tongue coming out of a mouth, extends and extends until it reaches Stanley.

"Come, come, Earthman, come and become the destiny of your kind."

Stanley stands and steps onto the offered ramp. The ramp retracts and takes him into the craft. With a gentle whoosh, the vessel shoots up and is on its way back into Outer Space.

2

*I*t had been a hard-fought battle for the high school football state championship. Each team had scored in brilliant plays, each team had their star player—beautiful examples of sweating human bodies—and the score was tied. Tied! The suspense laid thickly upon the crowd of humanity in the stands.

"Push 'em back, push 'em back, Waaay back! Push 'em back, push 'em back, Waaay back," the cheerleaders of the team on defense cheer in their flying-skirt outfits and big smiles and pretty faces. "Push 'em back, push 'em back—" The ball is snapped, the quarterback receives, the teams scramble with purpose, the ball is thrown, and— "INTERCEPT! INTERCEPT!" The star player of the other team catches and runs and runs and runs— "YAAAAAAAA!!!! Touchdown! Touchdown!"

One cheerleader, blonde and bouncy, turns to another cheerleader, petite and perky, and says, "Isn't he great! Isn't he great!"

"And he's sooo cute!"

"And sooo smart!"

"And sooo cool!"

"Captain of the football team AND its star player!"

"President of the student body!"

"The only son of the town's richest man!"

"Everybody loves him!"

"I—I—I love him!"

"What do you mean, you love him? He's mine!"

"Oh, yeah? Has he asked you to go steady?"

"Not yet. But he will."

"Well, until then, he's fair game."

"You stay away from him!"

"I will not!"

"Yes, you will!"

Petite and Perky jumps up and onto Blonde and Bouncy, bringing them down onto the turf. They roll to the right, they roll to the left, they roll to the right, slaps are exchanged, slugs are delivered, hair flies, tears stream, and screams of two tones dominate.

Red, green, yellow, blue; red, green, yellow, blue—coming, streaming, flashing, swishing light, dominating out the white light of stadium illumination, prepares the crowd for the landing of a spacecraft of no known human design.

Players scatter off the field, and the craft lands on the fifty-yard line. Scores of open mouths suck in the night air.

A voice fills all heads with words. A voice not human; words not English. And yet, all the heads are comfortable with them. And all heads understand them:

"People of Earth! Be not afraid. We are here to give, not to take. To heal, not to harm. Your brother, known to you as Stanley Lewis, has been with us, has learned from us, and has received wisdom and

powers far beyond any mankind has ever known. We return him to you as a Megaman, dedicated to protecting and nurturing your race in preparation for you joining the multitude of life in the outer reaches of space. Follow him. He now knows best!"

A sound both mechanical and biological sings to all heads as a door in the craft opens, and a long ramp, like a tongue coming out of a mouth, extends and extends. And on the tip of that tongue stands the Stanley that was, the Megaman that is. He is tall now, with a body newly muscled and is costumed in a red and blue, form-fitting suit of strange material. It is accented, quite naturally, with a flowing cape that flutters.

The crowd, quiet with awe, elevated with joy, feel as if they are floating, happy for this wind of change to take them as it will.

The star player who had intercepted the football and carried it in a rush to a touchdown—is compelled to advance toward Megaman with that prolate spheroid. He approaches slowly, with reverence, taking off his helmet and dropping it on the ground. He spits out his mouthguard and holds his head up high until he reaches Megaman. He then bows his head and falls to one knee and, with two hands, raises up the great football, that desired object of quest and conquest, and offers it in tribute to the wonder before him.

Standing on the sidelines (although they feel centered and whole and reborn), Blonde and Bouncy & Petite and Perky turn to each other to share the moment.

"Isn't he great! Isn't he great!"

And he's sooo smart!"

"And sooo cool!"

"Everybody loves him!"

"I—I—I love him."

"What do you mean, you love him? He's mine!"

"Oh, yeah? Has he asked you to go steady?"

"Not yet, but he will."

"Well, until then, he's fair game."

"You stay away from him!"

"I will not!"

"Yes, you will!"

Petite and Perky jumps up and onto Blonde and Bouncy, bringing them down onto the turf. They roll to the right, they roll to the left, they roll to the right, slaps are exchanged, slugs are delivered, hair flies, tears stream, and screams of two tones dominate.

Megaman sees this and is amused by the frail and fragile and faulty humans, and he cannot help but smile over that, but he must put a stop to it.

"People of Earth! Please—please—it is unbecoming for you—

Color drains away. White and gray and craters and mare pass below. With deep concentration, Lunar Module Pilot Buzz Aldrin watches all —landscape and instruments and history—and speaks to Neil Armstrong, Commander of Apollo 11.

"Two hundred feet...four and a half down...five and a half...nine forward...forward...picking up some dust...faint shadows...drifting to the right a little...drifting to the right...contact light!"

"Houston, Tranquility Base here. The Eagle has landed," Armstrong reports.

Touchdown! Man on the moon! Super historical; Mega monumental!

"That's one small step for Man, one giant leap for Mankind."

+

The students just don't give a damn. In fact, they don't even give a tinker's damn, not that they have any idea what a tinker is.

But Stanley gives a damn. Stanley gives a good goddamn.

"He blew it! Did you hear that? Neil Armstrong, highly trained military man, test pilot, engineer, astronaut, the All-American First-Man-On-The-Moon, sent there at the cost of millions and millions of taxpayer dollars, decides to make a momentous statement for history marking the exact moment Man fulfilled a centuries-old, nay, a millennia-old dream, AND HE BLOWS IT! 'That's one small step for man, one giant leap for Mankind' just does not make sense! As Armstrong stated it, 'man' and 'Mankind' are synonymous. So he is saying that 'man' and 'Mankind' simultaneously took a small step and a giant leap, all at the same time, which just simply does not make sense! Now, what he was supposed to say, and what he now claims to have said—even though this recording proves his claim false—is: That's one small step for A man, one giant leap for Mankind. Now that makes sense!"

A female student, sitting straight up in her chair but feeling as if she had been lying on the rack being tortured, whines, "Mr. Lewis, who cares?"

Stanley turns to her. He has never liked her. Even though a teenager blooming with youth, her whole being prefigures her middle-aged motherly self. "Who cares? The most momentous moment in the history of Mankind, and he blows it, and you shouldn't care?"

"Nah, big deal!" A male student, ugly of face as it has taken a few blows in amateur boxing and with thick dirty-blond hair slicked back, slouches in his seat and declares, "That all happened a long

time ago. It doesn't mean anything to any of us. People don't go to the moon anymore."

"Yeah," the pretty one, popular but bored with it, says, *"it's stupid!"*

R is confused, lost, and does not like it; it feels too much like being out of control. "Wait a minute!"

"What?" Stanley asks, not happy to have been interrupted.

"Are you still in high school or teaching here?

"Teaching."

"Well, you're leaving out a bit in the telling, aren't you

"Like what?"

"Like, how did high school end for you?" S asks.

"It ended. What else matters?"

"What about your grades?" T wants to know.

"No shame. No pride."

"And you went on to college," T notes.

"Yeah. Walked in the door, sat down, put out minimal effort; got a minimal education in return."

"But you got your teaching credentials," R reminds Stanley.

"Sure."

"So you must have done better in college than you are portraying here."

"Mediocre. That's all that was called for. That's all most children in America deserved. I became a Social Studies teacher. Back in the high school I had attended. I taught a succession of dull, bored, materialistic, self-centered, drugged-out, smart-assed generations of teenagers, each a *dee*-generation of the previous. Brilliance would have been wasted on them. Even competence."

R and S and T look at each other. R and T lean in from the right and the left to S in the middle. Their heads are put together—which Stanley finds disconcerting—and they confer. Eventually, Cerberus splits, and the three are whole, individual entities again.

"And, the moon…?" T asks.

"What?"

"What were your feelings, during this time, regarding the moon?"

"So, we're starting to pay attention to the moon, are we?"

"At your insistence," S says, on the edge of annoyance. "Why don't you be pleased instead of snide?"

"Snide? I haven't had anybody to be snide to in a long time. I guess I'm just stretching my snide muscles. Enjoying a snide moment. Allow me that."

But T isn't prepared to allow Stanley anything. "So, what was happening with the moon?"

"Well, in the period of my going from high school to— high school, Man went to the moon. It was the last mort-gage payment on Kennedy's eternal flame. It got a lot of press. So, in a way, I didn't feel alone anymore. Left out, but not alone. Then men stopped going to the moon. Just like that! One day we lived in the future. The next day we fell back into the past. We started confining ourselves to the relative safety and security and stupidity of low Earth orbit, tooling around in our big space truck. And *I* was ridiculed for my *taxi*? Jesus Christ, it was retarded! It was backward! We had made a move toward something, a movement that eventually could have included me, and then stopped, turned tail, and went the other way. Shit! *That's* stupid!"

"Mr. Lewis?" A snotty male student calls for Stanley's attention
"What!?"
"Did you hear? They're going to send a teacher into space
"What?"
"Yeah. that's what the news said," a sincere female student reports
"They want to send a civilian up on the shuttle, and the president said it should be a high school teacher."

"Yeah, you're always saying you want to go to the moon," the first female of her class to lose her virginity says, "maybe it can be you."

"Yeah," the male has a bright idea. "Maybe you can get a ride that far—and walk the rest of the way!"

The students laugh at such cleverness being manifested in the classroom, and laugh, and laugh, and...

"Well, the shuttle was stupid. But—but, okay, not to the moon, I understood that. It wouldn't be to the moon. Not there. But also not here."

Stanley sits right down and types himself a letter.

Dear NASA:
Why would I like to be the teacher chosen to fly a mission on the Space Shuttle?........

No, not right.

Dear NASA:

Why would I like to go into space? Be-
cause--I--want--to. What other possible
reason or desire do I need? Must I give you
some goody-two-shoes reason to impress
you? Must I throw in some patriotism or a
basic confirmation of this administration's
policies to attract your attention? Must I
be media attractive? Well-spoken? Propa-
gandistic-ally minded? Well, I'm not that
complex of a creature. I'm very simple, really. I just want to get my fucking feet off of
the Earth! I just want to be up there instead
of down here. I just want to touch the edge of
everything else!!! And, most of all, I want a
clear and unobstructed view of my--of the
moon. Which is actually where you should be
offering to take me. Why? Why, for god's sake,
are you guys wasting time skimming space
when you should be penetrating it! Get in
there! Explore! Expand! Why are you pussyfooting around? Have you no cocks, for god's
sake? You wimpy grandmothers! You should
all go to hell! It would be the only exciting

adventure you would ever have!
Sincerely,
Stanley Lewis

"I thought that such a frank and honest approach might open some eyes."

The NASA Administrator sits in his office from which he administers. A neat office, full of bright light and filled with models of spaceships—historical, on-the-drawing-boards, hoped for—and with pictures of space, space explorers, one U.S. President, and three family members. He picks up the three thousandths two hundred and thirty-second letter he has considered. The previous three thousand two hundred and thirty-one were all fine, nice, safe, obvious. But this one, he starts to perceive as his eyes scan back and forth, this one...

"Whoa, what have we here! Jesus, you can feel this man's passion radiating from the very paper of this letter. This guy is a natural. A space child destined to conquer space. And he's right, he's right, damn it! Why are we wasting our time in low Earth orbit? Call the President, damn it! I've had enough of this pussyfooting bullshit! We're going back to the moon! And Mr. Stanley Lewis is going to lead us there!"

"You never got a response to that letter, did you?" T slices with a sharp-edged query.

But Stanley feels no pain; he just shakes his head. "Nor to the eight follow-ups. It was a *very* conservative administration."

Various voices of dedicated men and women fill the air and the airwaves.

"Three, two, one...Liftoff of the 25th Space Shuttle mission...And it has cleared the tower...Challenger, go at throttle up...Roger, go at throttle up...."

FIREBALL YELLOW; BALL OF SMOKE WHITE!

"Flight controllers here looking very carefully at the situation. Obviously, a major malfunction ...."

"Gee, just think, Mr. Lewis," the male student with the almost square head and freckles says, "it could have been you."

The chuckles and giggles from the boys and girls in the classroom are like the little spitballs Stanley had suffered for years.

"Shut up," Stanley says quietly as he continues to watch the screen on the big TV on the big cart which had been rolled into his social studies classroom, especially for the launch. But that only boosts the chuckles and giggles to laughs and guffaws. Stanley turns to his students and roars—"Shut up!"—and leaps to the male student and pulls his head up by the ears and brings his own head down, and shouts and spittles into the student's face. "SHUT UP! She died— trying to get into space—just to teach a couple of school lessons—to the likes of you!"

"I quit teaching," Stanley says.

It is a matter-of-fact statement. R and S and T feel no need for elaboration.

Besides, Stanley seems somewhere else. "Where to go? What next?" Stanley seems to be asking himself.

The comic collector had been collecting comics since he was a kid. He's now an adult, full of enthusiasm, if not social graces. He's on the hunt. He has heard his prey might be at booth #32 in the dealers' room. He walks up to it cautiously as he has heard that the man in the booth isn't the friendliest of individuals. He scans the offerings on display. There! And—and, there! "How much for the Flash of Two Worlds?" The comic collector asks the man in the booth, who is staring out at the many milling and flowing motes of humanity, passing judgment on each and every one of them.

"Seventy-five dollars," Stanley answers without looking up at the comics collector.

'With what savings I had, I opened a comic book store specializing in comic books and science fiction and fantasy. I called it SPACER'S HAVEN."

"Uh-huh," the comics collector says, contemplating, calculating. "And the Hawkman number one?"

"A hundred and a quarter."

'Some of your business is conducted at comic book fan conventions—Spacer's Heaven. Haven or heaven, both are nothing but extensions of every little nerd's dusty bedroom where they sit and stare at color panels depicting the colorful adventures of colorfully costumed superheroes battling just as colorfully costumed supervillains in conflicts boldly black and white."

"Hawkman's not that popular!" The comics collector is aghast.

Stanley does not give a damn. "He is with me."

'The heroes are all sculpted physical specimens of perfect form. Their worshipers—for that is what they are—their worshipers are almost all fat or skinny, tall or short, often ugly, and—on occasion—lame."

"But the Flash is a classic."

"Fine. A hundred and fifty for the Flash."

"At first, I thought I would be comfortable with these people. We shared. We understood. We were alike. But I soon tired of the reflection. If that is what I looked like— then I did not like to look."

"No, I mean you can't charge more for the Hawkman than you can for the Flash."

"Why?"

"You're way off from what the buyer's guide says."

"I set my own prices."

"But the Flash—

"The Flash is a red-suited clown, and I hate him. Whereas Hawkman has the elegance and grace of natural flight and only his wits and strength to defend himself with. He is a super person, not a super being!"

"Oh, okay—a hundred and twenty-five for the Hawkman."

"But I was successful! I made more money catering to the needs of nerds, their need to deny the blandness of re- ality, than I ever did, or could have, trying to teach the facts, the this is so, the here it is, the way it is, the just plain IS of the world instead of the IF."

Stanley stuns himself with the profundity of what he has just said.

"Yes, that's it! Nerds need IF, have got to have IF, are addicted to IF, desire IF, fight for IF, would die for IF, but become distracted when you dare mention the IS. Don't you see how I became disgusted with IF and wanted to find my way to IS?"

"Hey, Stanley, do you want to go to the Moon?"

"YES!"

"Great! Can I borrow some money? I blew all mine in the dealer's room. 'I will gladly pay you Tuesday for a hamburger today'."

"The Moon was a little coffee shop that became our haunt, our joint."

Stanley walks into The Moon coffee shop with a young woman prettier than she has a right to be. She looks better in her Wonder Woman costume than the nine other fans at the convention who have also made and donned the Amazon's signature look. Also with him is a falling-into-middle-age man carrying a huge, stuffed bag over his shoulder that he often smacks people with when he turns to his right or turns to his left. He seems not to know how to say, "Excuse me." They are lucky, a booth has just become available, and they grab it. The Moon is owned by a man who believes deeply in themes and atmosphere. He has always cared more for the design of his shop than the quality of his chops. The owner finds no fun in feeding faces and cleaning up after them. Still, he enjoys immensely the mounting of large astronaut-photographed blow-ups of moonscapes. Wonder Woman and Bagman has never known how much the blow-ups had Stanley's attention and how little attention he has paid to them.

A mother-waitress comes over, thick of waist, blue of hair, tired of customers. "What'll ya have?" She demands to know.

Wonder Woman looks at her menu and begins, "Ahhh—I'll have the Crater Burger, Firmament Fries, and a Moonglow Satellite Shake."

Bagman continues, "I'd like the Earthrise Surprise, over easy, with a double order of Landing Pads with the Selene syrup."

They wait for Stanley to make up his mind. "I—don't—know. I'd like a Mare Melt with Sub-orbital onions, but jeez, that sounds so heavy. You know, maybe I should just have a fruit salad."

"We don't have fruit salad," mother-waitress says.

"You don't?"

"Of course not—there are no trees on the moon."

"Oh—of course not. Well, how about Sea of Tranquility Soup? That is, if I remember, in Earthling language, chicken noodle?"

"With or without gravity?"

"Gravity?"

"MSG."

"Oh. Without, please."

"It was at The Moon that I realized I was soon to be an old man. At least, that's what I thought at the time. Actually, I was only reaching middle-age. No—pre-middle-age. You see, I was turning fifty. Fifty! A half-century old! Jeez, dig the grave; make it comfy; I was ready. But that was *over* a half-century ago. Modern medicine—isn't it great! Most people don't have lives worth living, and those bastards go about extending the insult."

"Time slowed?" S, who somehow knows, asks.

"Oh, yes," Stanley admits. "Time slowed. With nowhere to go, your only trip is through time. Always traveling steady and slow. No speed limits needed to be posted. No cops needed to enforce. There was no gas to hit."

"So you just kept selling comic books?"

"No. I retired. I made a nice little bit in the care and feeding of nerds. I had made investments. I was—secure."

"Where did you retire to?" T wants to know.

"My moon room. A friend once called it my mushroom, "...for you sit like a toad on a stool in there." A former friend, I should say. No friends now."

Stanley stops and withdraws for a second or two in real-time, but who knows how long in his time. Then he comes back.

"It was a windowless room of four nice walls that I covered with huge blow-ups of astronaut-photographed moonscapes." Stanley looks around him. Stanley is there. "I tried to make this enough."

What views is he looking at? What plane? What side of a crater? What rocks?

"Then—the ultimate insult."

"I am delighted to announce that the President today has instructed NASA to begin preparing for America's return to the moon."

"After all those years! The great ugly monster of opportunity."

Voices—voices stab at him with some delight.

"What opportunity? They're not going to let you go to the moon. What chance have you got?"

"They will take selected civilians along," Stanley thrusts back.

"Oh, bullshit! Sure, some have gone to the space station, but that's nothing anymore. This is a dangerous mission; you know what happened back in '86."

"'86 was many years ago."

"What makes you so sure then?"

"Simple. We have found profit in Earth orbit, but a slim slice of

the total. Now the moon beckons. It will take money. Money takes votes. Votes come from civilians. I am not a complete dreamer, you know."

"You were right."

"Oh?"

"The President has announced that there will be a civilian on the first NASA return flight to the moon."

"Yes?"

"She has decided it will be—a poet."

"Oh."

"A poet? Well—why couldn't I become a poet? I certainly had the leisure for it. I didn't have much time, though. They would choose the poet in ten months. I had to quickly become a bright new light in the poetic firmament. I had to start writing. But what? I figured something nice. A committee would make the choice, so I figured that it had to be something nice. And sweet. And lovely. Sigh producing stuff, probably about birds and the power and beauty of flight, especially as a symbol of the soul ascending.

"I got in my car and drove up to the mountains and started to commune with nature. Nothing. I hated it. Got bit by bugs. Got into my car and drove down to the ocean. Awful. Seagull crap on my windshield. Got into my car again to go home. Shit! I came to a stoplight. Shit! I saw something, and I just started to think of words. Shit! They weren't what I wanted to write, goddammit! But they stayed with me all the way home. And, goddammit, I wrote them down!"

It was another hall, a lecture hall. Where this time? A library? A college? A university? A civic center? Not a bookstore. No halls in bookstores. Bookstores did not like Stanley Lewis, the poet. Not him alive and aloud, while sensitive souls who did not ask to be abused by him were present picking up their thrillers and their romances and their how-to books. They might overhear him, off in a corner of the bookstore with unfolded chairs before him, some butt-filled, some not. All seats, installed, folded-down, were mostly butt-filled here in this hall somewhere in the landscape of his wanderings.

The host makes introductory remarks, mentions the bursting-onto-the-scene that marks Stanley's story. A Cinderella story of sorts. Or a sordid Cinderella story? Finally, he says, "Please welcome, Stanley Lewis."

Applause, some polite, some curious, some enthusiastic, greets Stanley as he comes up to the lectern and, without preface, begins.

"What a pleasure it's been
To piss in porcelain!
It's never dull
To face a urinal.
It's quite a rush
To come before a flush.

And to sit
(Like on a cloud)
On a padded ring,
With that scented thing
Stuck to the wall,

What a ball!
I mean it's fun.
And when the do-do is done,
You get to wipe it
With a softi,
What a lofty
Experience.

It really was a boon
For Mankind
(Kids and women, too)
When they made the verb 'to defecate'
Not only an active, but graceful state,
In which to sit and meditate
On the past, present and future fate
Of Mankind
(Kids and women too).

I mean before you simply sat,
Did your business, and that was that.
Except to clean yourself - by hand
(A filthy practice, you'll understand).
Later, of course, they had catalogues,
Sears and Wards
And those other dogs,
With pages packed
With products to buy
(The frilly stuff made the ladies sigh).

But what really mattered
(Besides the bell-ringers)
Was, properly used, they kept feces from fingers.

And isn't it quite fine,
Don't you think?
How we have competently
Covered up the stink?
Pink is the color our upstairs is done in,
Even the bowl we drop our dung in

You see, Mankind
(Kids and women too)
Has come a long way.
It's true—life's one big fray,
It's small and mean and mundane,
It's petty and dirty and insane,
But take your pipe and put this in:
Although man is a beast,
At the very least,
He has a
Clean, shiny, soft, sweet-smelling
Pot to piss in!"

"I take it that poems like this," says R, who is very good at stating the obvious, "did not get you to the moon."

"No," Stanley smiles as a puff of breath comes out of his nose. "They did not get me to the moon. But they did make me a celebrity of sorts."

"A celebrity?" R is incredulous, possibly aghast. "You were an odd little man spewing out clever vulgarity, and that made you a celebrity?"

"Yeah. Do you understand how that could happen?

"No, I do not."

"Probably some weird tick leftover from the 20th century. All I know is I became a cult figure. And I went around the country reading in lecture halls and classrooms in major and minor colleges to major and minor people who seemed to me to be nothing more than variations on the theme of comic book fans. Nerds of another color. Geeks of another stripe. Granted, I was having fun. The baby loves his screams; the child loves his tantrums; the adult loves his art. But it was not getting me to the moon. The chosen poet was a big, strapping, no-hint-of-homosexuality guy from the Northwest who wrote about birds and the power and beauty of flight, especially as a symbol of the soul ascending. Big fucking deal!"

S possibly sees the sadness in this—and perhaps does not. "So this poet got to go to the moon?"

"Yes. This poet. Then a photographer for National Geographic. Then a painter. Then a documentary-novelist. Then a video artist. Then a whole fucking improvisational stage company. Then a housewife. Then a blind paraplegic. Then an idiot savant. Then three six-graders from the Nancy Reagan Middle School in Anaheim, California. Then a mother and a child. Then a boy and his dog. But *never* again a teacher. Then Congress appropriated billions and billions of dollars, and citizens stopped going, and industry started, and the military started. And then there were mines on the moon. And manufacturing plants. You could buy products stamped: MADE ON THE MOON.

"People were going to the moon. People who had never wanted to go, people who had never dreamed about going. People who couldn't begin to *be* on the moon the way I could *be* on the moon. But I couldn't be on the moon. I didn't want to be a miner. Products made on the moon were made by machines. I certainly didn't qualify as a warrior. A certain commercial venture would bury you on the moon, but they required that you be dead before they would take you up there. There were hints that commercial travel to the moon would soon be a reality, but as it was going to be extremely expensive, and as they had not yet built a Holiday Inn on the moon, what was the use? I was—as I often had been and seemed destined to continue to be—depressed."

Stanley lowers his head in a perfectly depressing attitude. Then raises it back up and shows R and S and T a perfectly scary smile.

"And then they built a prison on the moon."

The mall is massive, gigantic, huge—pretty damn big. All the delights of America to be had for a price under one roof. He felt it to be fortunate that he had found a parking spot close to an entrance. It meant a shorter walk as he sported unconcealed empowerment: an assault rifle, two semi-automatic handguns, and a long hunting knife in a leather sheath strapped to his right leg. He dashed into the entrance, right by the food court, and was immediately assaulted with the smell of chocolate chip cookies. Standing there before him, in a cute little gold and purple uniform, was a cute, petite teenage girl who held a tray of cookie samples in little white cups. She innocently offered him one. He shot her dead in the middle of her forehead. There was a moment of silence except for the reverberation of the shot—then the screams began. He walked calmly and casually, scanning the field before him, moving his eyes to the right, to the left, dead center, then scanned again and again. With the assault rifle, he spread out a bunch of hot projectiles into the Beans and Bacon Eatery, splattering beans, bacon, and brains. He looked at the mini version of a Hamburger Peddler, a fast-food chain prolific throughout America, indeed, throughout the world. He was convinced their fatty, fat-causing, fat-headed food was one of the leading causes keeping Earthlings rooted to the planet. POW! POW! POW! Three shots. Three burger slingers dead. Earthlings were everywhere in the food court, cowering under tables. He laughed. He could quickly kill their appetites. But there was more to life than just food, and he moved on into the mall proper. There was a super large sporting goods store, brightly lit with intimations of sweaty muscle burns, selling oh so much stuff, many things he had never had a need to buy. Two-fisted semi-automatic pistol reports shattered the store's large, look-in-and-be-envious windows. Then he walked in and sprayed bullets everywhere, more interested in shooting things than people. Still, people got in the way and became things. As he walked out, he grabbed a football as his trophy. He continued down the mall to the central hub of it all, to the elegant escalators. As he moved up with the escalator, he could hear sirens, cops, the fuzz, law enforcement. He assumed they were coming in vehicles of great muscle doppler-ing down the street, lights rapidly flashing and blinking all at the same time, all in acknowledgment—if not celebration—of him. He looked down upon the Earthlings below, cowering-cowering, shaking-shaking, afraid to rise and be counted. At the top of the escalator stood a little girl, maybe four-years-old, abandoned, or forgotten, or escaped from her parents. He took out his very long, sharp hunting knife and lopped off her head, which bounced-bounced-bounced away like so many of the balls she had played with in her short past. To his right was an obese man, a big round thing with pudgy appendages holding his breath in fear. He shot him in the chest. And the held air escaping through the tiny bullet hole sent the fat man flying up. Up and away, dashing and fluttering through the air until he hit the high glass ceiling, then fell down with a splat. To his left was a very skinny man, a wimp, shrimp. He sent a bullet his way and it missed, as did the next one and the next one. So thin and hard to hit. Finally, he got him, and the bullet split him like a reed. The right half and left half of the man fell away from each other and fell flat on the floor. The sirens were getting louder now. He saw a high-end clothing store for female Earthlings. Life-size, life-like, statue-like representations of the currently perfect female form were in the window. They all wore delicate clothes that only the finest of their species were allowed to wear. He walked into the store. There was erratic sobbing, panicked crying, and terrified screaming coming from somewhere he could not see. But that did not matter, for he was not concerned with them. Instead, he shot to pieces the life-like, life-size, statue-like representations until they were piles of flesh-colored rubble. As he walked out of the store, he heard heavy, manly voices shouting out orders, commands. So what? He silently questioned as he continued on his way, racking up more deaths, wiping out poor weak Earthlings. Until he felt he had done enough, according to his plan. Then he stripped himself of all weapons, stripped himself of the military camouflage fatigues he had bought on the Internet. Stripped himself even of all undergarments until he was completely naked. He then fell to his knees and put his hands behind his head, as he had seen count-less times on TV.

MAD POET IN KILLING SPREE—17 DEAD

"MR. LEWIS!" R was irritated.

"What the hell are you upset about?" Stanley asks. "Scenes like this have been part of our popular entertainment for years!"

"Mr. Lewis!" R was pissed. "I am sick and tired of these fictions! The one thing we did know about you when we came up here is that you killed no one! Now—what was your crime?"

Stanley gives R and S and T a bizarre grin as he lowers his chin with chagrin. "I could have killed—murdered—slaughtered. Really, I could have." Stanley raises his face and puts it forward to R and S and T. "But the idea was such a cliché. Everybody was doing it! Besides, I didn't have to kill anybody. I could do the next best thing to homicide. I could destroy property!"

Stanley jumps up, excited, like during a major holiday. "Something big. Something built at enormous expense.

Something—something people took great pride in. I blew up—"

Stanley twirls once. "Oh, it was incredible!"

Stanley twirls twice. "Stupendous!"

Stanley twirls three times as if he is going to break into song. "A massive orange fireball in the night shooting up, toasting my skin, bringing a glow to my face like I've never had! I blew up the brand new, recently built at great expense, focal point of civic pride, Los Angeles Museum of 20th Century Popular Culture!"

MAD POET BLOWS UP LA MUSE OF POP CULT NO ONE INJURED

Stanley sits in his defendant's chair. His public defender (who could find no public defense for Stanley) sits next to him, dreaming of a French Dip sandwich at a particular restaurant in downtown L.A. The judge is high up on his bench, preparing to read his sentence. Very high up sits the judge, so high a little white cloud has formed above his head, making Stanley think of British judges in countless movies and TV shows. He would not be surprised if the sentence is read in a clipped and crisp British accent. But it is not. The judge reads in a flat, characterless, monotone drone.

"Stanley Lewis, you have been found guilty of felonious destruction of property by a jury of your peers—twelve nerds good and true. Do you have anything to say before I pass the sentence?"

"Well—do I get to go to the moon now?"

"Stanley Lewis, throughout this trial, you have shown no remorse.

Have you no conception of the magnitude of your crime? You destroyed the repository of the very essence of the very soul or the very spirit of America. Popular culture, by definition, defines us. Therefore, it was us you blew up."

"Well, actually, I was just going to blow up the Comic Book wing, but I guess I used too much explosive."

The judge pounds his gavel; the wood on wood slam reverberates, echoes, pierces, wakes up a woman in the third row.

"Stanley Lewis, I hereby sentence you to life imprisonment at the Lunar Correctional Facility in the Sea of Tranquility, Moon."

Stanley smiles, oh does Stanley smile, smiles so broadly his cheeks become two happy points of pain...

Stanley screams, "NOOOOOOOO!!!!!!!"

Stanley is strapped to his seat in the prison transport rocketship; an IV needle has just been inserted into his arm, the drip has started.

"NOOOOoooooo!!"

The voice of a young female adult of official resonance says, "I'm sorry, but those are the regulations. 'All prisoners shall be anesthetized during transport to the moon.' Now just relax and let the drug take effect...."

"No!" Stanley struggles against straps. "No!" Stanley's struggle subsides. "Nooo, ah, oo...." Stanley sleeps.

Stanley awakes, groggy. "Whe—where am I?"

A pleasant, motherly voice comes from the ceiling. "The Lunar Federal Correctional Facility, Sea of Tranquility, Moon

"When—when will I be able to see?"

"See? See what?"

"The moon. The—the lunar surface. The blue of the earthrise."

"Well, you don't. I mean, we're three kilometers inside a mountain and two kilometers below the surface. This is, after all, a maximum-security prison."

"You mean there are no windows to look out? To see the moon's surface?"

"No, of course not. We do have an earth environment simulation for exercise and to combat de-rootedness. But we have no system for allowing prisoners to look out at the moon's surface. Why would you want to? There are no trees on the moon."

"AAAAAHHHHHHHHH!!!!!!!!!!!!!!!!!!!"

"So—" There is something in R's voice. It causes S and T to whip their faces toward him, to observe everything about him as they listen to his voice with its timbre of triumph, with the color of confidence. "So, here you sit— *supposedly* on the moon."

"What?" It is like a kick to Stanley, a kick while down.

"Well," R says, getting up from his chair and walking around the bare room. "You have absolutely no empirical evidence that you are on, or, rather, to be strictly accurate, *in* the moon. So this great goal of yours that has informed your life, that has shaped your whole being, here you sit, thinking you have achieved it, but you don't really know that—do you?"

"This isn't fair!" T stands up and declares, stopping R in his tracks.

"What?"

"This isn't fair. You are goading the man."

"I'm sorry, did it seem that way? I thought I was just

making a point."

"No! You were driving home a point to try to get him to do what you want."

"So?"

"So, it's unnecessary. We have a fair bargain to strike, a simple bargain. Offer it to the man. But don't try to manipulate his behavior to get the acceptance you want."

"I resent what you are saying."

"Oh, come on!" S intercedes to clear the muck. "You are a manipulative son-of-a-bitch, you've always been a manipulative son-of-a-bitch, and this is just further proof of it."

"*Who* is the leader of this team?" R puffs out the question.

"A position you did not deserve but got by manipulating people."

"You have made that charge before, and I have successfully defended myself, must—

"Please!" T follows her exclamation with a slam of her open hand upon the tabletop. "None of this is germane to the matter at hand. The only thing that matters is whether Lewis is a suitable candidate or not. What you see in him that has led you to this shameless manipulation is exactly what I see in him that would lead me to declare him unfit. He would not be able to make a rational decision."

"Well, yes," says S, the only one of the three still sitting. The only one of the three not agitated. "But on the other hand, I don't think we should lose the opportunity that Lewis potentially provides."

"And may I ask," R tamps down his anger but stokes his frustration, "how many more of these interviews do you want to go through?"

The subject of this heated exchange, yet a man forgotten, speaks. "Did I fade into the background or something?"

"What!?" R says, irritated by the buzz.

"What!?" T says, just as irritated.

"Am I not here anymore? Did someone send me out of the room and not tell me?"

S, the calm center of the room, answers. "Mr. Lewis, there is an experiment we want to conduct."

"An experiment?"

"We are looking for a suitable candidate."

"Suitable for what?"

"For volunteering."

T sits down. R returns to his chair. It is time to be attentive—a delicate time.

Stanley looks down the row from one to another. From R, with a gaze demanding a conclusion, to S, with a smile and encouraging eyes, to T—she's rather attractive, Stanley finally notices; in a marble sort of way. "Are you," Stanley addresses them, "*mad* scientists."

There is a short HA!, a titter from somewhere, and a jaundiced guffaw. Which came from whom, Stanley cannot tell.

"No, no, Mr. Lewis," R says. "We *are* scientists, that we will admit to, but we are certainly not 'mad'."

"I meant 'angry'."

"What?"

"I meant 'angry.' Are you angry scientists that you had to come all the way up here to the moon to find your volunteers?"

"No, Mr. Lewis, we are not angry," S calmly says, soothing, she hopes, any concern. "Our research has to do with the moon."

"Oh. Finding out more ways to exploit it, are you?"

"Yes," R is happy to admit, proud, in fact, to confirm. "But I wouldn't put the negative connotation on the word that you put on it. The moon has absolutely incredible potential for manufacturing, mining, the military—

"Manipulation?"

"Mr. Lewis! Just hear me out. That great potential is not being reached. Why?"

"Bureaucratic bungling?" Stanley offers. "Mischievous mismanagement? The desert years in American education? The sour and cynical motivation that emphasizes exploitation over exploration? The—

"Mr. Lewis! If you shut up for one moment, you will find that I am in a position to offer you what no other man, and certainly no god, has deigned to offer you. I am your only hope for personal fulfillment. I am the only source for your happiness!"

"Stop it!" T rises and screams. "You have lost your objectivity in this matter!"

"And you have lost your job!"

"You can't—

R stands and chases T. "Get out of here!" Around the room once, twice—"Get out of here right now!"— and out the door, echo sounds from a long hallway flooding in until R slams the door shut again. He turns to S. "Are you with me in this?"

S considers her position, then says,

"For the time being. But if it goes wrong, I will claim I was coerced."

"It will not go wrong," R says as he swings around to face Stanley. He looks at him intensely. Stanley looks right back. Then R walks to him and bends just enough to be more face-to-face with the seated Stanley. "Mr. Lewis— how would you like to take—a moonwalk?"

"What?"

"It is not what Stanley expected, not that Stanley expect- ed much.

R pushes his face closer to Stanley's and speaks in a steady, quiet, yet vibrating tone as if something was build- ing up.

"How would you like to go up that elevator that is just down the hall, the one you have not ridden since the day you got here? How would you like to go up that shaft that you have only come down in? And how would you like to —not only look out through the one small window that is up there, out to see the surface of the moon—but to actu- ally leave this facility and walk out onto the surface of the moon, and *be* there—as only *you* can *be* there?" R unbends, backs up, smiles, raises his right hand, and rests it on his upper lip as if he were an artist contemplating his creation.

Deep inside Stanley, confusion churns, curiosity rises, cynicism slices. "Is this—torture?"

S, calmly, starts to reassure, "Mr. Lewis—

"Is this part of some new form of punishment? Are you going to let me go up there and look at the moon and then pull me back at the last moment? Are you—

"No!" R, emphatic, punches the word at Stanley to stop him. "No, Mr. Lewis. We are actually going to open the door and let you walk out."

"What did I do? Win a contest I did not enter? Is this for good behavior I have not displayed?"

"We are not doing it for you, you crusty old bastard! We are doing it for us! To benefit from our pure selfishness, you just have to say yes."

"Yes!"

S is disturbed over Stanley's quick acquiescence. "Mr. Lewis, you don't quite know—

"Shut up!" R turns on S. "He said, 'Yes!'"

Excitement, something Stanley has not felt in a long time, good-naturedly slaps him on his back, ejecting him from his chair. "Su-sui-suit me up! What are the suits like now? Are they lighter? Are they—are they now designed for greater mobility?"

R, a self-satisfied smile spreading on his lips, is happy to report that, "You won't—need a suit—Mr. Lewis."

"Uuuuuhhhh!" Stanley's realization of the only possible

answer is swift and stinging. "You terraformed the moon! Didn't you, you bastards!? You brought up fucking trees!"

"No, no, no," R is quick to answer. "Calm down! We didn't terraform the damn place. Too complex, too complicated. We went for the simple, the elegant. A serum. The 'Shirtsleeves Serum.' One injection, and you can walk out onto the moon in your shirtsleeves—and survive! You can walk out onto the surface of the moon as if you were taking a walk to the corner mini-market. It does three things. Controls body temperature: no matter if it is frigid or boiling on the surface, your body maintains a perfect 98.6. Second, conserves oxygen: one deep breath before you step out, and you're good for twenty-four hours. And, finally, combats radiation: You won't even need a hat! All-purpose; super strength; three-in-one!"

Stanley thinks of the possibilities, the ease, the comfort. He quickly unbuttons the front of his sickly green jumpsuit, extricates his torso and arms, and offers his right arm to R. "Shoot me up!" Then, thinking of another option, he pulls the rest of his jumpsuit down to his knees. With a flourish, he presents his moon on the moon. "Or do you want to do it in my ass?"

"The arm will be—

"Mr. Lewis," S helps Stanley pull up his jumpsuit with a gentle tug and guides his arms back into its sleeves, "what you don't understand is that this is experimental. It has never been tried on a human before."

"I don't care," Stanley says.

"He doesn't care," R says.

"You could die," S warns.

"I don't care," Stanley says.

"He doesn't care," R says.

"Mr. Lewis, don't you even want to know what you get for volunteering?" S asks.

"I know," Stanley says with a deep and personal understanding.

"*He* knows." R says as if it is the word of God, a word before which one should show respect and remain silent.

But S insists. "Mr. Lewis, if you volunteer and survive, you will be granted parole and returned to Earth."

"Don't tell him that!" R shouts at the blaspheme.

But Stanley is not disturbed by the crudeness, the vulgarity—the earthiness. "Well," Stanley says, "I guess that's just the price I will have to pay." He offers his right arm once more. "Shoot me up!"

R gladly obliges by sticking a long needle into Stanley's right arm, then plunging the shirtsleeves serum into the blood coursing through one of Stanley's veins. Then he reaches into his briefcase and brings out a small ear canal implant. "Mr. Lewis, I want you to wear this."

"What is it?"

"It's a communication device. It will allow us to talk to you while you're out there. I want you to report everything to me, everything that you feel. Also, we are going to implant in your skin—

"Ouch!"

S has slipped a miniature monitor with one sharp edge under the skin on Stanley's neck. "Oh, that didn't hurt, did it?"

"We've implanted a small device that will monitor your body functions and transmit them back to us," R explains. "Temperature, oxygen content of your blood, that sort of thing. Do you understand what we want from you while you are out there?"

"Can I take that chair?" Stanley says, pointing to the chair he has been sitting on.

"The chair?" R asks, trying not to scream at the absurdity of the request. "What do you need the chair for?"

"To sit on."

"Mr. Lewis, there are plenty of rocks out there—

"I would prefer the chair."

R hates impediments, hates roadblocks, hates naysayers. R hates Mr. Stanley Lewis. But hates even more that he needs him. With a sigh, he turns to S. "Can—can we let him take the chair?"

"Gee, I don't know. It's property of the prison."

"Well, can you ask somebody?"

"Well, if I ask somebody, we're probably going to have to fill out forms. Do you want to have to fill out forms?"

No, no, R does not; that is the last thing he wants to do. He turns to Stanley with a plea in his voice, and had he not had two emotionless ocular implants, he would have puppy-dogged his eyes. "Mr. Lewis, do you really need to take the chair?"

"I can't see myself going out there without it."

"Oh. Um, well—

"I'll just take the chair, okay?"

"Yes—fine—take the chair."

Stanley picks up the chair. A fine, institutional hard metal chair. But in one-sixth gravity, no burden at all.

"Are you ready, now?" R asks.

Stanley looks at R deeply. "When have I not been?"

+

Stanley takes the long elevator trip up alone. He would not have taken the trip at all if he had died in the elevator, for it was an airlock elevator. This two-for-one innovation had saved much money and burnished the reputation of an administrator. But he did not die. He took in his big breath, then R and S sucked the air out of the airlock. Outside the airlock elevator, looking in at Stanley through a small window, R and S held their breaths as well—but Stanley was fine. He was smiling. He was furiously pointing up—up! R and S, outside the elevator, sighed out their breaths in relief. Stanley, of course, did not. He kept his breath held, as instructed.

When the elevator gets to the top, the doors open, and there—there—Stanley can hardly believe it, there is the moonscape. A brightly lit ground of variations of gray, dented and battered and strewn with rocks and here-and-there boulders.

Stanley, still in his sickly green prison jumpsuit and carrying his chair, leaves the elevator, leaves the side of a mountain, and walks—lightly, of course—onto the surface of the moon. He is struck by the short horizon, sharply delineated from the deep black sky. A short horizon? Why is he surprised? He has seen countless astronaut photos of the moon's surface, all with short horizons. But that is seeing, not experiencing. Not experiencing the irony that the moon has always been his far horizon, and here he is, having finally reached it, left with a short horizon.

Still, he can jump higher than he ever has before, and he does, once, twice, a third time, covering much distance, he and his chair. Finally, he settles down, setting the chair down. He closes his eyes. He opens them again. No, the moon is still here; he has not been dreaming. He looks up. Well! Why hasn't he noticed it before? There is the Earth— a bit blue, a bit brown, a bit white.

An annoying buzz comes into his ear.

"Mr. Lewis? Mr. Lewis?"

It is the annoying R.

"Can you hear me?"

"Yes, I can hear you."

"Mr. Lewis, how are you feeling right now?"

"I feel—wonderful!"

"Yes, yes, Mr. Lewis, but that's not the point. I want specifics. Are you warm or cold? Do you feel a shortness of breath? Do you feel any nausea?"

"I feel out of breath."

"Out of breath? But—but, Mr. Lewis, our monitor indicates that the oxygen level is holding in your bloodstream—

"Out of breath with wonder!"

"Ah, well, yes, Mr. Lewis, I am not looking for poetry here. I'm looking for data. Now, what do you perceive the outside temperature to be?"

Stanley sits on the chair, looks around, perceives—feels. "The climate is calm. And so am I as I sit here on the bank of the river that flows through our small town."

"Mr. Lewis! Please! Now, does it feel like 70 degrees out there? Or 80? Or 90, perhaps? Your body temperature is holding at 98.6"

"No!"

Another buzz in his ears, a sharp buzz, a buzz on alert.

"What?"

"It's going up!"

"What?"

Stanley leans back in his chair and extends his legs, crossing them at the ankles. "It's a warm night here in the city. Some relief can be had, though, sitting here on the front stoop of the old brownstone."

"Shit! Look at the drop in oxygen content!"

"Mr. Lewis?" S buzzes in his ear with concern. Concern for him? Concern for the experiment? Concern for the chair?

"Mr. Spinelle, the grocer, walks by." Stanley waves to the translucent grocer walking in and out of small craters. "Hey, Mr. Spinelle!"

"Is he delirious?" Buzzes S to R.

"I don't know. Mr. Lewis, tell me how you're feeling. Mr. Lewis?"

Stanley jumps up and starts to walkabout. "Stubby! Stubby!"

"What? What's he talking about?" The little voice of R lodged in Stanley's ear asks. "What's a Stubby?"

Paper flips rapidly, "Stubby—Stubby," back and forth, "Stubby—stubby," then the flipping stops. "Ah, here it is. His childhood cat. He thinks he's a kid in his backyard looking for his cat. Mr. Lewis, I think something's happening. I think you should come in now."

Lewis spins around and faces the side of the mountain. "Ah, do I have to come in now, Mom?"

"Yes, Mr. Lewis—Stanley," mother S says, "please come in now. I'm very concerned here. We are getting abnormal readings. You are abnormal, Stanley!"

"Just a few more minutes, Mom! Pleeeeeease!"

"Damn!" Bursts out R. "Now his temperature is dropping. I don't understand these wild fluctuations."

"We've got to get him back!"

"Just a few more minutes, please. I want to track these fluctuations."

"He'll die."

"What?"

"He'll die!"

"Oh. Yes, of course. Ah, Mr. Lewis, you better come in now."

Stanley says nothing and makes no move, except with his eyes which pan the moonscape.

"Mr. Lewis? Mr. Lewis, come in now, or I will have to send somebody out there to—

Stanley pulls the implant out of his ear and flings it away, sending it up into a long, slow arc into the black sky and back down to settle in moondust.

"Mr. Lewis! Mr. Lewis? Mr. Lewis?"

Stanley walks to a large boulder about the size of his bing childhood home. He hops up to the top, plants his legs steady on the flattest area, and stands akimbo under the glowing blue-brown-white Earth. "I fly up here as often as possible. To be alone. The demands of Earth are much for a superhero. Saving every life you can. Fighting every evil you find. The constant, clutching demands from the poor, weak Earthlings that depend on my strength—

Why would you want to go to the moon? There are no trees!

Stanley looks up at the Earth in explosive anger. "You don't understand! It's not about trees! I think I shall never mock a tree as lovely as a rock!"

That's stupid!

Stanley cringes, bringing his eyes down to look over the vast—but with a short horizon—multi-shaded gray, blemished moonscape. He takes in a sudden, strained breath of horror and asks himself what he has never before asked himself:

"What is in my soul that I find *this* beautiful?"

What is in my soul that I find this beautiful?

What is in my soul that I find this beautiful?

What is in my soul that I find this beautiful?

What is in my soul that I find this beautiful?

But he looks again at the moon, the quiet, unchanging, relatively eternal moon.

"No, not beautiful—comfortable." And he becomes as

calm as the moon itself.

Stanley leaps off the bolder and leaps-leaps-leaps, back to his chair, his hard metal yet comfortable chair. He sits. He shivers.

"Gets a might cool out here in the early evening this time of year."

Stanley vigorously rubs his arms, then crosses them. For warmth? To defy?

"That's okay. I'll just sit here until I become *too* uncomfortable."

In the distance, behind him, at the foot of the mountain, the elevator doors open and out walk two spacesuited individuals. They spot Stanley, point, and come toward him.

Stanley does not know this. Stanley only knows the moon and the chromatically more complex bauble in the black sky. And to the bauble, he says:

"You see—I had wanted to come to the moon from the time I was an infant."

STEVEN PAUL LEIVA

WHAT A PLEASURE IT'S BEEN TO PISS IN PORCELAIN

The Rude Poems of Stanley Lewis

Assuming you have already read *Made on the Moon* you will have noted that its protagonist, Stanley Lewis, had once been a poet of some fame and/or infamy, depending on how you feel about poems about birds and the power and beauty of flight, especially as a symbol of the soul ascending. Following are some of his poems.

STEVEN PAUL LEIVA

CONSIDER THE PLIGHT OF UGLY PEOPLE

Consider the plight of ugly people
In a world gone giddy for glamour.

Consider their world creamed with beauty,
Thick, rich, sweet, but beyond their taste,
Their tongues lapping, their lips feeling only
The milky thin, their cheeks filling only with lumpy
Curds.

Consider the plight of ugly people
As they encounter their enemy, the mirror.
Consider the revelation of reflection, the pain of light,
No joy, no flight, no pleasure in person.

Consider the plight of ugly person Sara,
Over thirty, thirty over,
Surrounded by the beauty that escapes her.

Consider her actions, day to day, night to night.

She smokes, of course, as ugly people do
In their subtle search for glamour.
She holds it thus, and sucks it swell,
And blows it out with style.

Consider the makeup she buys,
Enticed by ads
Glossy, flesh tone, red on high cheek bone,
Blue on languid lips.

Consider the monthly magazines she buys or barters,
Trading them for others others have bought,
Mother brought a stack today.

Consider their names: GLAMOUR, of course, and
BEAUTY
And VOGUE and REDBOOK
(REDBOOK? What the hell does that mean? Oh, well,
Consider—they never put ugly on the cover.)

Consider her reading room, bare ass stuck in hole
Over tidi-bowl
As she turns pages to see what sages
Will reveal that will peel off pounds of ugly flesh
Or what
Mixture of magical chemicals with exotic and erotic
names will work their will on William, and make him
Forget her
Hook nose, buck teeth, big ears, and lack of chin.

Consider Sara dabbing makeup, but it's yet to shake-up
Her basic components and rearrange then into
Pretty or cute or attractive or beautiful or
Any other combination but ugly.

Consider Sara's defense—self-deprecating humor.
"Beauty may be skin deep," Sara says with a sigh,
"But who wants to date sinews and bones."

Consider the plight of ugly people
As they watch 5, 6, and 7 O'clock news,
And see the world through eyes so fair, hear it through
Smiles so sweet or sexy or sensually serious
When death is announced.

Consider the newscasters stuck in radio—betcha they're
Ugly.

Consider the plight of ugly people
Faced with the fact each shopping day
That department store dummies are prettier than they.
Even the ones with no faces.

Consider Beverly Hills, where ugly people are
Stopped at the borders.
They are shot on sight.
Their skins are used for Gucci shoes.
Consider the rich, who are always beautiful.
It is always "The beautiful rich," or "The glamorous
Rich."
It is never "The ugly rich."
Except to Socialists, of course.

Talk about ugly! Lenin was ugly. Debs was ugly.
Emma Goldman was really ugly!
Beatty as Reed was beautiful,
But that's Hollywood for you.

Consider romance novels and their handsome heroes
And beautiful heroines.
Consider their readers—ugly women in dull towns
Picking their noses as the villain picks a fight.

Consider the benefits of beautiful booze to ugly people.
It's a billboard transformation, they hope,
Into Black Velvet or black tie, and yet
Consider—ugly girls go out together,
Ugly men hit the bars in pairs.

Consider the plight of ugly people.
Their only hope is age, where ugly becomes interesting.

Consider death to all beautiful people,
To make the world fair for the ugly.
Consider gassing them, or charging their beautiful bods
Full of numerous volts. Why not?
They don't have the votes.

We have tried to eliminate, eradicate minorities before.
Beauticide's the answer, shove them through the furnace
Door.
Bring purity to the species, pure ugliness for all!

No—forget it. Won't work.
No one wants to see the beautiful dead.
No one wants to give up the cream
Set so high on the shelf.

There are anti-intellectuals—the dumb disliking the
Smart.
There are anti-fine—the crude disliking the sublime.
But who is anti-beautiful?
The ugly love what they are not.

Consider the plight of ugly people
In a world gone giddy for glamour.

CLOSE CALL FOR FOOTBALL

The kid kicks the football
Up over the fence
Swiftly up
Small arch
Down fast
To
Bounce, bounce, bounce
Onto Santa Monica Boulevard
Car swerves
Look!
God!
Up
Over curb
Into fence
Another car
Scared
To the left
Into oncoming
Traffic
Of course
A crash

Metal gives
Compresses
Presses
Into flesh
Bones break
Blood is misdirected
Death follows

The football goes unharmed.

YOU POMPOUS ASS SON-OF-A-BITCH

"You pompous ass son-of-a-bitch"
You accuse me of being,
But my being has never denied it.
"You pompous ass son-of-a-bitch"
You insist.
As if by telling me you'll change me.
As if revelation will reform.
But what have you revealed?
What eyes have you opened?
What deep soul shame do you
Think you have spawned with
Your little barren verbal sperm?

You tell me nothing I do not know.
You draw no curtains.
You open no doors.
You shed no light.

What right?
What claim to shame?
What "Pity the poor boy, let's improve his lot"
(What rot!)
Powers do you assume
Are yours by some grace of DNA

That compels you to impale me
On some self-righteous lance—

Look.
Listen.
Try to understand.

That I am pompous is a
Fact not a fault.
I admit it,
But I don't submit it
For your review.
I suppose I respect your view.
But not much.
For it always looks out, never in.
So I don't have time for it.
For I intend to win.

I have had to look in.
And see and surmise and summarize
And categorize and quantify
And qualify and list and
Label and like and despise
And regret and revel in and
Be pissed and be pleased and
Love and have to laugh,
For I am such a silly God
Damn ninny at times.

But they are my times—
Tick-tock—
My sixty seconds per minute,
My sixty minutes per hour,
My hours, my days, my weeks
My months, my years, my story,
My life, my being,
My self,
My center.
I do not need you to enter.
So get, scoot, scat!
There are no faults in my character,
Only facts.

OLD LADY CAUGHT

Old lady
Caught in a crosswalk
Running to reach the other side.
The green had betrayed her,
Allowed the red its time.
But her time,
A long time,
Is not over yet, she feels,
So she peels out
In a flatfooted prance,
A flight for survival dance,
Holding up one HALT! hand,
Hoping the tonnage to stand,
The speeding to stop.

It's ludicrous.
Hit the gas and the old lady's smashed,
Crushed and creamed,
Flattened and spread out
In a flesh and blood dream
Of what once was a beauty
Of maybe grace,
A pretty face,
A passion expressed in moans and screams,

A mother tender,
Or a terrible bitch,
A person of wisdom
Or stupidity which
Added nothing and made no note.
So write her off and ride her over.

She makes it.
She hops with short breaths upon the curb.
I did not dare to disturb
The fragility of her flesh.
I did not break her bones.
I did not draw her blood.
I did not scatter her life
To the winds, back to the elements.
She cried for survival,
She strived for survival,
And won, age no factor
Against the tonnage.
She won.

This time.

FAT MADONNA WITH CHILD

Fat lady in the park,
Gross and gargantuan,
Full of flesh
Puffed out,
Rounding her out,
As if the inflation ring had been pulled.
Is there air between
Her skin and bones?
If so, stale.
But probably rather rancid
Meat, dark red with
Things interior crawling
And potential stench appalling.

Fat lady's face
Is big beach ball-like.
A beautiful bounce,
If one could detach it.
A rapid roll,
If one could bowl it.
Her eyes floor tiny craters.
Her nose marks a tiny spot.

Her mouth neither smiles, nor frowns,
But flares out loudspeaker like,
Projecting petals of flesh
Projecting peals of invectives
As crude and coarse sounds
Emanate from her to her
Child.

She is a mother.
A collaborator in life giving.
A womb holder and protector.
A fluid giver,
Nourishment provider,
Gene depositor,
And blood transfuser.
She opens her legs to drop child.
She opens her arms to greet child.
And finds the bundle a burden.

The child grows and spreads out,
Becoming a slice of her,
Or a reduction print copy
from the original.
Small instead of big.
Male instead of female.
The child is called Charlie,
"Charlie!" is the call of the wild

Fat lady, always, it seems, ready
For high-pitched screams
That batter against his head
Through to the final dread.

Death
Is offered up with glee,
If not seriously.
But how does the fat
Little kid know that?
Mother, madonna, maternity,
Marvelous?
What if Mary had been a bitch—
A mother ejecting,
A parent rejecting?
He may not have been
Such a damn nice guy.

NOTHING MAKES ME HAPPIER
THAN A DEPRESSING DAY

Nothing makes me happier
Than a depressing day.
I mean,
When the sky is gray,
Tending towards black,
Textured, layered,
Patterned by some
Master of chance
With winds river strong,
And not to be denied,
Their shadow streams
Kicking leaves around
Down here among the rooted.

I can see better
In the gentle light,
The not so white,
Diffused through the clouds,
The harsh filtered out.
It falls upon the earth
Less stringently,

Allowing me to see
More lovingly.

The cool of such days,
Kiss my skin,
Sweet and simple and moist,
With a bit of breath added.
I find myself hugged
By shirt, sweater, jacket,
Comfort coming
From warm and cool mingling.

My mind,
Like man-made computers,
Hates the heat,
Loathes the street burning,
The pavement reflecting,
As I walk, thought
Trying to push through,
Desiring the cool,
Where connections are made,
Where conceptions are laid
Out to see, to view for value.

To walk under cloud cover,
Streams of winds passing,
Gentle light descending,
Reflecting smoothly,

Cool caressing,
Caressing contrasting warm.
Steps on ground.
Steps of contemplation, Steps going forward…

Nothing makes me happier
Than a depressing day.

SUMMER BEACHES, WINTER BEACHES

I wrote this title down
Some time ago.
It sits there on top of this page.
I hate it!
What the hell did I have in mind?
Some poem of comparison
Between the
White and hot
And the
Grey and cold?
Between the
Crowded and confused
And the
Sparse and simple?
Some stupid lines
About the soul deep gray
Drama of one alone
On the beach feeling
The elemental waves
Inevitably pounding
Out beats, metronome-ing
The rhythm of life,
That great mysterious
Clockwork under-reality

Of all we see, that,
Mystery or not,
Everyone feels compelled
To write about, and comment on,
Because—face it—
We all love a mystery?
And was I going to
Compare that with
The thousand-fold beaches
Of Summer, where slick
Bodies, various bags
Of flesh, cavort upon
The sands—sit, lay, swim,
Dream of sexual intercourse,
Or the results of a barbecue—
Amid beachball bright colors
And carbonated drinks, not
Paying attention at all
To mysterious deep rhythms, nor
Caring to, for the Frisbee
Is in the air and they
Must catch it?

No—I cannot possibly believe
I was going to write such a poem.

I HAVE NEVER BEEN TO WAR
A Civilian's Lament

I have never been to war.
Never.
I have never seen action.
Never.
I have never raised a rifle
In anger
And rarely in play.
I have never shot hot lead
Into the flesh of my enemy
Nor separated his meat from his
Bones with a bayonet.

I have no camp tales to tell.
No laughs over beers.
I have no buddies from that time,
Friendships forged in battle
That I see now and then.
I have never gotten VD
From some nameless woman
Speaking a strange tongue
Who I consciously screwed
Despite the lectures
Because I was thinking with drink

And was so lonely
I thought I would die
My genitals would dry.

I have never had my picture taken
In dress uniform and sent it
Home to mom to rest
On the mantel.
I never saw that same picture
In the local herald, heralding
Me as PFC.

I never flew to a foreign
Land in the service of my
Country.
I was never a lonely boy
Away from home.
I have never had coffee and
Donuts at the USO.

I have never been to a camp show.

I have never been on a game show
In Hollywood, on leave in
Uniform, buttons shining,
Hair short, the host proudly
Clapping me on the back.
Back home the aunts
All a twitter as I win

250 dollars.

I have never received dangerous duty pay.
I have never received disability pay.

I have never driven a jeep
Shirtless, hat askew, butt
Hanging from my lips.

I have never read Stars and Stripes.

I have never hated my sergeant,
Or respected the "Old Man,"
Or cursed any officer behind his back.

I have no material for a novel.

My father never went to war.
4F,
He was an air raid block warden
During WWII with few
Stories to relate.

My father had nothing to tell me about war.
I have nothing to tell my son.
I have nothing to pass on.

I have nothing to add to the
History of Warfare.

SADNESS OF AN ORDINARY MAN

Where is my importance?
As I walk through the art gallery
To look at the work of the
Recent great man
And read of his greatness
Which makes his importance
On big cardboard panels
Displayed on the wall.
And see photographs of
Him in black and white
Images
Of obvious importance.
You can tell that.
Importance has a magical effect upon
Emulsion.

Where is my importance?
As I attend the theater,
Identify myself by the tickets
I've bought, ceremoniously
Ripped in half as I am
Directed to my seat my
Hands stuffed with the Playbill

—read it and weep—
That lists the important
Accomplished actors and others
By lists of
Their important accomplishments.

Where is my importance?
As I walk down Madison Avenue
Window shopping, being loving
Or critical of things I might
Or might not be able to afford.
As I come across many cops
Alert but not worried and
Notice in the distance
The spinning red replacing white,
White replacing red lights of
Slowly oncoming
Official vehicles.
"What's happening?"
"The Chinese premier is visiting
New York."
"Oh."
Cop cars pass as various smudges
Of American human life stand
And turn to watch as the
Black Limousine passes with
The grinning Chinese premier
In the back seat as more

Cop cars pass.

Where is my importance?
As I walk into the men's store
To buy a belt and tie tack
But flirt with the clerk
Making him think I'm ready to
Buy, buy, buy
—as I am used to usually doing—
But let me think about it first.
"I may be back tomorrow."
For this coat and those pants
And several flannel shirts besides
Just in case I'll need them,
Just in case the weather turns cold.

Where is my importance?
When they give speeches
Accepting the Oscar or Tony or Emmy
Illuminated by lights loyal
Not just to the interested audience
But to the integrated circuits
Thanking and smiling and basking
As I might do later to
My just windexed bathroom mirror.

Where is the importance
Of being an observer

One of the audience
A stand in
A stand by?

Where is my importance?
Where is my center stage
Forum
Podium
Spotlight
Close-up
Captioned photo
White lettered name superimposed
Over my video image
Open mike
Unauthorized biography?

Where is my importance?

REFLECTIONS UPON SEEING
A MOTH CAUGHT

I suppose poems about
A moth
(Or some such insect)
Caught in a spiderweb
Have been written before.
But I've never seen it before,
So indulgence is due.

I am not a great observer
Of nature.
My eye is not keen to the
Little dramas
Among the
Little creatures
Played out on a
Little patch
Of this
Little planet
Lost in a great
Big universe.
I have rarely reflected
With Thoreau-like care
Upon the never ending cycles
Of seasons,

And thus the
Birth-Death-Rebirth
Favorite litany of
Sensitive souls.
Or on the beauty to be found
In the shells or trails of snails.
I hate snails.
Except with garlic.
But I forget the moth.

On the balcony of a motel
I saw a moth caught
—or possibly existentially entangled—
In the web of a spider,
The malevolent spinner of which
Stood nearby.

The moth furiously beat his wings,
But
The moth futilely beat his wings,
But
What else could the moth do?
It couldn't think his way out of
The situation.
It couldn't talk its way out of
The situation.
And it certainly couldn't take it
To litigation.

It had but one option.
And that option was doomed to fail.

The spider just sat there.
No, stood,
Stood is what I said before.
Stood, I'm sure.
A spider has eight legs
—even I know that—
And it has no rump
—as far as I can tell—
So it must have stood.

[Pause for reflection]

Yes—stood!

The spider just stood there,
Master of his lair,
Waiting for his supper
To settle.

Should I continue to stare,
Waiting for the inevitable
To happen?
For the moth to exhaust,
The spider to stir,
As cruel Nature decrees

The horrible in-aracnidian event
To occur,
Stirring my poetical impulse
To dash down some
Lesson learned,
Wisdom received,
Revelation revealed?

No—no time.
I'm hungry and hanker
For pig meat,
The sweet pork flesh
Of my fantasies.

"Pork chops, please,"
I ask of my waitress,
My web.
And she brings them to me
Prepared and pretty,
Laid out with pineapple,
Potatoes on the side,
And the innards of pea pods.
Piping hot coffee washes it down
After devotional devouring.

Spiders know no such service.

PLEASE FEEL FREE

Please feel free
To rake my emotions
To gather together the leaves,
The myriad variations of
Love and hate,
Pain and Pleasure,
Joy and Sorrow,
Grand ideals, or
Petty concerns.

Go ahead and gather
Them up into a pile
So you can take then in
And comprehend them as a whole,
Making a thing
Out of a universe.

Be my guest,
Run, leap, and fall
Into them,
If you insist on being a child,
Crushing some,
Scattering others.

No thanks necessary
If
Instead
Being an adult
You set fire to the pile
Burn each leaf
Ashen my emotions to
Particles even smaller
More fragile and insubstantial
Than they were when you found them.
Make yourself at home.
I'll clean up afterwards.

I WOULD LIKE TO TALK IN RIDDLES

I would like to talk in riddles
And rear my ugly head
And thoroughly confound the masses
As I talk to them from the dead.

I would like to leave off failing
Each time I put foot forward
And lay in the grave with grapes
Groping for one more word.

I would like to like the quiet
Then I would punch and cut the drums
And move my ass for no one
Except other bums in slums.

I would like to know the meaning
Of so many lines of verse
And cheat the frantic fate
Of the pen and paper curse.

WHAT A PLEASURE IT'S BEEN
TO PISS IN PORCELAIN

What a pleasure it's been
To piss in porcelain!
It's never dull
To face a urinal.
It's quite a rush
To come before a flush.

And to sit
(Like on a cloud)
On a padded ring,
With that scented thing
Stuck to the wall,
What a ball!
I mean it's fun.
And when the do-do is done,
You get to wipe it
With a softi,
What a lofty
Experience.

It really was a boon
For Mankind
(Kids and women, too)
When they made the verb 'to defecate'
Not only an active, but graceful state,

In which to sit and meditate
On the past, present and future fate
Of Mankind
(Kids and women too).

I mean before you simply sat,
Did your business, and that was that.
Except to clean yourself by hand
(A filthy practice, you'll understand).
Later, of course, they had catalogues,
Sears and Wards
And those other dogs,
With pages packed
With products to buy
(The frilly stuff made the ladies sigh).
But what really mattered
(Besides the bell-ringers)
Was, properly used, they kept feces from fingers.

And isn't it quite fine,
Don't you think?
How we have competently
Covered up the stink?
Pink is the color our upstairs is done in.
Even the bowl we drop our dung in.

You see, Mankind
(Kids and women too)

Has come a long way.
It's true—life's one big fray,
It's small and mean and mundane,
It's petty and dirty and insane,
But take your pipe and put this in:
Although man is a beast,
At the very least,
He has a
Clean, shiny, soft, sweet-smelling
Pot to piss in!

STEVEN PAUL LEIVA

CYRANO DE BERGERAC AND BARON MUNCHAUSEN GO TO MARS

A Short Story

This story was written for the anthology of short stories *Turning the Tied*, published in 2021 by the International Association of Media Tie-in Writers. Cyrano de Bergerac (1619—1655) and Hieronymus Karl Friedrich, Freiherr von Münchhausen (1720—1797) were both real individuals and fictional characters. Cyrano de Bergerac actually was a famous swordsman and author of one of the first works of science fiction, *The Other World: Comical History of the States and Empires of the Moon.* Hieronymus Karl Friedrich, Freiherr von Münchhausen or Baron Munchausen was infamous as a teller of outrageously tall tales at dinners he hosted. Cyrano was fictionalized by French playwright Edmond Rostand in 1897. The Baron never wrote down any of his tales, but tales attributed to him were published by a series of writers. They were not "licensed" to do so, and the Baron was not happy about this. Nevertheless, is it possible that these scribes were the very first tie-in writers? It is to wonder.

STEVEN PAUL LEIVA

1

FRANCE 1641

Savinien Cyrano de Bergerac, a young member of the King's Guards, sat in his cups after several cups of a not very distinguished wine in a little tavern in a not wholly decadent section of Paris, but certainly not a dignified one. It was close to the theater where Cyrano and two of his fellow Guardsmen, the twins François Jacques and Jacques François, had spent the better part of their evening. François and Jacques tried their best to lighten Cyrano's mood. For, besides being in his cups, Cyrano, his head buried in his folded arms on the table, was in a morbid melancholy.

"Cyrano," said Jacques (unless it was François), "you are the most irritating guardsman of my acquaintance."

"Mine too!" François said (unless it was Jacques).

"You had a great triumph tonight. You bested and mortally wounded a great swordsman in a duel of honor at the theater. And this while still suffering some pain from the neck wound you received in the Siege of Arras. It was *Spectaculaire!* (Which, of course, means Spectacular!) *Magnifique!* (Which, of course, means Magnificent!) *Affreux!* (Which means Awful! But in this case, "full of awe" and not "objectionable," for obviously François—or Jacques—was not objecting). "It will only enhance your repute, your fame, your legend!"

Cyrano moaned and slowly raised his head, bringing into the tavern's low candlelight and fireplace illumination his *spectaculaire*, less than *magnifique* but certainly *affreux* nose. He looked at the twins, his fellow men-at-arms, and said in a slurred voice, "I would rather be known for my rapier wit than for my rapier." Then he dropped his head back onto his folded arms.

"You see," said one of the twins (we will dispense with trying to figure out which), "that is your problem, my friend. You care more for your books, your poetry, and mooning after your cousin than defending France and your honor with your incredible talent with the sword."

"Some talent," Cyrano said, raising his head again, his face mapped with disgust. "Sticking pigs! And what a pig he was! Not just of the body but of the mind. How did he insult me? Was it at all clever? Was there some felicity to his words? An apt way to offend me? No, just your mundane, *'Mon Dieu, mais tu as un gros nez!'*" (Which means, "My God, but you've got a large nose!" But it sounds better in French). "Oh, if only I had answered back with some wit, some poetry, possibly with how he could have cleverly insulted me if he had not been a witless dolt. No, I just answered with the inarticulate clang, clang, clang, clang of metal! Oh, why do I always think of the witty things to say, the beautiful *bon mot*, after the duel?"

The twins looked at each other and shook their heads. They had heard all this before; they understood Cyrano"s anguish no more than they ever had, and it was boring. Time to pick up their friend, plop his white-plumed cavalier's hat onto his head, and escort him home.

But Cyrano did not want to go home. Despite their objections, he bid farewell to his friends and took himself off to his favorite bit of countryside nearby.

There, along a lonely road, stood a single spike-like Italian cypress tree that he felt to be his friend. For it stood as oddly in this landscape as Cyrano did in the Guards. He loved to sit under it at night and look up at the sky, especially on a night like this, a night of a full moon.

The moon, the moon, Cyrano thought as he stared directly into the moon's man-like face. Earth's companion in the sky. No, not just a companion, but a brother. What are you like, brother? Who resides there, brother? What are your secr—

A wispy cloud appeared before the moon. Which was odd because it was a cloudless sky. But, no, it was not a cloud. It was a supplanting face! Transparent at first, moonshine flowing through it, it slowly came into solid integrity. Cyrano soon realized that standing before him was a man, strangely dressed, wearing an odd triangular hat and sporting a broad, cheerful grin, and... and... and...

"*Mon Dieu, mais tu as un gros nez!*" Cyrano said as he looked up at the man

2

THE MAN IN FRONT OF THE MOON

"Yes," said the elegantly if strangely dressed man before him. "It is a magnificent nose, is it not? A real Hanover hooter! It flows freely from out of my face and curves down quite beautifully, the whole forming an aspect like the side of a gently rolling mountain. I am quite proud of my nose. Although, I suppose the pride actually belongs to my progenitors. But be that as it may, allow me to present myself, I am Hieronymus Karl Friedrich, Freiherr von Münchhausen. But you may call me Baron Munchausen!"

At any other time, being presented with such an aristocratic fellow, Cyrano would have jumped up and shown due respect with a flourish of a bow. But he was perfectly comfortable sitting against his cypress. And he was not entirely convinced he was not dreaming. It seemed the better course to stay as he was. Still, apparition or not, Cyrano needed to address the stranger. "Am I correct, sir, in assuming you are a citizen of the Holy Roman Empire?"

"Ha! As your fellow countryman Voltaire will someday say, it is neither holy, nor Roman, nor an empire."

"Will *someday* say?"

"Yes, he has yet to be born," the man in the triangular hat said offhandedly. "I prefer to say that I am from Bodenwerder in the Electorate of Hanover. But that is just Geography, my friend. More to the point, I am from the future! 1790, to be specific."

"I must," Cyrano said as he dropped his head and shook it to reorder the confusion within, "I really must stop drinking cheap wine."

"Oh, stop whining about your wine, and stand up, man, and embrace me, for we are fellow authors!" Baron Munchausen scooped Cyrano up as if he were but a child, a small child, possibly, even a rag doll, and brought him into the fellowship of his arms.

"But... but... I am not an author," Cyrano said once the Baron had released him.

"You will be, my son, you will be."

"No, no, I am a King's Guardsman, a swordsman, a man of duty and honor."

"Poshtiddle!"

"Poshtiddle?"

"You will quit the guards this year and begin studies with Pierre Gassendi."

"Gassendi? The philosopher?"

"Yes, yes! He will tickle your mind as he opens it, and then you will write poetry, plays, and prose. And you will write about going to the moon!"

"Going to the moon? I was just thinking about the moon."

"Who doesn't think about the moon? So obvious, so mundane, even I have written about going to the moon. But now, I could truly go there."

"What?"

"And I could take you."

"What?"

"But, I will not!"

"For pity's sake, why not?"

"Because I have come here to take you to Mars!

3

BARON MUNCHAUSEN EXPLAINS HIMSELF

"In my time and world, I am known as *Lügenbaron*, The Baron of Lies!"

Cyrano's eyes flashed with righteous anger as his long, and promontory-like nose twitched in agitation, for he could always sniff out an insult. "What an affront! I would kill any man who disparaged me so."

"No, no, Cyrano! It is not an insult. On the contrary, it is a perfectly precise appellation. Indeed, a fine honorific! For I have told the most outrageous, ridiculous, absurd, unbe-lievably tall tales of any man living or dead. And yet people hang on my every word, often with the most beatific grins on their faces, enraptured with my lies; it would not be a lie to say. It has been a most pleasant occupation for me."

"But, Baron, to what purpose?"

"Why to amuse, Cyrano, purpose enough."

Cyrano looked down upon the ground and saw there—there being within himself—a truth. "Not for me."

"Yes, I know. You will put philosophy in your writing, the true nature of things, promoting ideas that will not, I must say, please your Church. But that is the nature of your essence. But I am here to inspire you to do it with some panache, some flare, some outrageous and glorious lies!"

"Here?" Cyrano questioned. "You have still not explained how you happen to be here, in Paris, in 1641, instead of Hanover in 1790."

"Ah! Yes, a strange and wondrous thing, that. I was walking one day in the mountains with a group of friends. They were hanging on my every word, as I told them of how one day when I was standing on the edge of the White Cliffs of Dover in the island kingdom across the channel, a lightning bolt shot down from the heavens and streaked through my legs—I was standing akimbo at the time—and snatched me up into the sky. I told them how I rode that bolt like I would ride a fine steed, all the way to the antipodes. Specifically, New Zealand, another island country, where I found myself in the company of a tribe of well-spoken koala bears. Just as I was beginning to elucidate on the koalas' customs and taboos, I was—truthfully, in actuality, very, very, realistically, and with great veracity—struck by lightning. It burnt my clothes and fizzed my hair and singed my nose, and I fell into a deep stupor. My companions transported me back to my hunting lodge—for that is where we were staying—and tended to me with great tenderness for the next forty days. During those forty days, I emitted an intermittent glow and, quite unconsciously, recited many of the works of Lucian of Samosata. Upon waking after forty days, I felt wonderful and saw no reason we should not carry on with our holiday. That night, my friends and I—there were five of them, aristocrats all—played a card game of English Whist. I was telling them of my great adventure in mid-Africa, where I battled an enormous crocodile. I bested him by reaching down his throat and grabbing the inside of his tail, and pulling him inside out. They were, of course, mesmerized by my tale, glued to their seats, as it were. Then all of a sudden, an enormous crocodile burst through the wall and gobbled up three of my five aristocratic friends."

"Stunning!" said Cyrano, who was sitting on no seat to be glued to but was mesmerized still. "Amazing! And tragic."

"Well, the three ingested ones were lesser aristocrats, whereas the surviving two were higher born."

"Are you saying their deaths were less tragic because of the position in society that their births gave them?"

"My dear Cyrano, there is a reason why the low-born are called the low-born."

"But my dear Baron, are we not all low-born? Wasn't it only Athena who was born high?"

After a short period of perplexity, the Baron got Cyrano's allusion to the ancient myth. He shook with laughter both Teutonically and tectonically. "Ah, you are clever with the words and ready with the wit, my fellow possessor of the proboscis colossal!"

By reflex, Cyrano shaded his nose from the moonlight as he lamented, "Oh, were that so, Baron, were it so. But forget my wit or lack of it. Are you saying you conjured up a real, living, enormous crocodile by your lie?"

"Yes, my friend, that is exactly what I am saying. I have become such a consummate liar, such a fabulous fabricator, that my lies can now become part and parcel of the fabric of the universe. I have but to tell them to make them real."

"That is—that is unbelievable!"

"So is the virgin birth, my friend, but..."

"But... but..."

"But how do you think I got here in an instant from Hanover—not to mention 1790? I just told myself the story of me being here—and I was here! I will prove it to you. On this lonely country road, I will lie up our conveyance to Mars."

"Would not the moon be closer?"

"Poshtiddle!"

"Poshtiddle?"

"The moon is but a low-born satellite, a servant of Earth, colorless, barren, and uninteresting."

"A servant? How does it serve?"

"By moving our ocean tides in and out, of course."

"Not according to Master Galileo."

"Master Galileo was right about many things but wrong about this. But that, my dear Savinien Cyrano de Bergerac, is not the point. Do you not realize that the Earth and all the planets are the children of mother Sun? That the planets were born one after another from her fiery womb and sent out into space? As Mars is farther from the Sun than we, then it must be older. It must have a civilization of peoples more advanced and mature than we. Think of the wonders we will find there, the knowledge we can gain."

"But what if it is like an older sibling happy to torture the younger?" Cyrano asked by way of warning. "It was, after all, named after the God of War."

"A mistake of antiquity, my friend! No, no, look at Mars! Not all white and pale like the weak moon, but red, sanguine, a good fellow, optimistic, I'm sure. But we can talk about all this on the way. For now, let me lie up our conveyance. I think I will use the chariot of Queen Mab that I featured in my tales of African adventures! Give me but a moment."

The Barron began to mutter, chuckle, and finally exclaimed, "The chariot of Queen Mab be here!"

And there, on that lonely country road appeared the most strange of all conveyances ever imagined by man. It was huge, a prodigious, globular coach that looked like a giant hazelnut, mainly because it was a giant hazelnut. There was a hole in the shell as large as a regular coach door, and the interior, which the Baron invited Cyrano to look in and examine, featured a luminous representation of all the stars of heaven. It goes without saying that Cyrano was amazed! But as I just said it—it's too late now.

Breathless, Cyrano backed his head out of the coach and stumbled backward to fall against his cypress tree, sliding slowly down the trunk to sit, composure having abandoned him. But it did afford him a full view of this wondrous mode of transportation. Nine bulls were hitched to the chariot of Queen Mab to provide forward motion. The lead bull was enormous, with horns that may have reached into the next district. Behind him were eight average size bulls, but positively not minuscule in bulk and strength. The bulls were shod with the skulls of men, which the Baron explained gave them extraordinary abilities to transgress any landscape. Indeed, any seascape, and—the Baron said it would soon be proven—space itself.

On the back of the nine bulls sat nine postillions, nine riders to direct the nine bulls, for there was no coachman to drive the chariot of Queen Mab. Just one postillion, seated on a lead animal, is normal, but having nine of them is not what was strange here. All nine postillions were crickets! The size of monkeys! Their chirping was loudly incessant, as you would expect of *Grylloidea* (in a story like this, it is always good to throw in a little Latin) of such inflated size.

"And now, Cyrano, get up and join me in the coach."

Cyrano rose in apprehension. "But will we be warm? I have heard that the higher up you climb the great Alps, the colder it gets."

"We will be perfectly warm, I assure you."

"And will we be able to breathe? I have also heard the higher you go in the Alps, the thinner the air becomes."

"Yes, yes, we will be warm, and we will breathe because I will lie us up some heat and air. If I have not convinced you yet, Savinien Cyrano de Bergerac, what more can I say?"

What more, indeed, Cyrano thought. He was not a young man of faith, except the faith he put in his swordsmanship, so how could he put his faith in this apparition from the future? Or this conjuring demon from the present? But because the Baron was imbued with confidence, and his offer of the most unique of adventures was strangely compelling, Cyrano got up and, with no hesitation, joined Baron Munchausen in the giant hazelnut, closing the coach door behind him.

"How long will it take us to get to Mars?"

"Who knows? No one has ever gone there before."

"Do we have provisions?"

"When I think, 'breakfast,' we will have breakfast. When I think, 'lunch,' we will have lunch. When I think, 'supper,' 'dinner,' 'dessert,' and 'wine,' we will also have those. And the best part is—there will be no washing-up afterward! Now, let us go on to Mars!"

Each monkey-size cricket on the back of each bull chirped louder and louder until the sound was almost deafening. The chariot of Queen Mab shook violently, tossing Cyrano and the Baron side to side until the shaking became an intense vibration. Then forward ballistic movement threw the men against their seat backs. The hazelnut coach sped faster and faster along the lonely country road. Finally, the massive bull in the lead leaped in a great bound up into the sky. They ascended at such an incredible rate, the Baron and Cyrano flattened like *Homo crêpes.*

4

THE TRIP TO MARS

They knew they had escaped the Earth's massive pull of gravity when they unflattened and recovered their fully dimensional selves.

"That was an odd experience," Cyrano said as his face took on a chartreuse hue, and rumblings in his stomach made an unpleasant prognostication. But the Baron simply lied about Cyrano's condition, picturing him as a fellow in fine fettle, and the future was bright again.

"Well, Cyrano, how should we pass the time? Shall we play cards?"

"I am not that fond of games, Baron."

"How about I regale you with some of my fabulous adventures."

"Meaning no offense, Baron Munchausen, but I think the fabulous adventure we are currently on commands our attention more, don't you?"

"How so?"

"Well, for example, I've just noticed that this coach has no windows. There is nothing to look out of, to see where we are, where we are going, or, for that matter, where we have been."

"What do you need to see, my dear Cyrano? We are in space somewhere between Mars, which is where we are going, and our mother Earth, which is where we came from."

"But wouldn't you love to see our mother Earth from out here? To see that it is a globe spinning in space."

"You don't believe it is? You need evidence?"

"Well, of course, I believe it. But just think what it would mean for all those less educated among our fellows if they could see it and be disabused of atavistic notions."

"Such as?"

"Such as that the Earth is flat."

"For most people, my friend, for all intents and purposes, the Earth is flat. Why try to unbalance them with details?"

"But, Baron, don't you think it would be fabulous for people to see the Earth in space? I'm pretty sure they would not be able to see our arbitrary and often disputed borders. If all people in the past had been able to see that we are all one people on one planet, I'm sure then I would not have suffered this neck wound while being a loyal French subject fighting just as loyal Spanish subjects at the Siege of Arras."

The Baron smiled a gentle yet somewhat patronizing smile as he said, "Ah, my dear friend, just because you cannot see the trees for the forest does not mean the bears are not shitting in the woods."

"What?"

"I would much rather muse on what we are going to find

on Mars. The possibilities are endless."

"*Oui! Oui!*"

"You need to urinate, Cyrano? Don't worry; I can just lie your bladder empty."

"No, I meant, in your language, *Ja! Ja!*"

"Just a little joke, my friend. In the future, *badezimmer*, or if you will, *salle de bains* humor will be quite the thing."

"I didn't know they had humor in Hanover."

"Ah, *Touche*, as you like to say!"

"But, to muse on Mars, yes, I think that is a fine idea. I am intrigued by this idea of yours that the inhabitants may have a civilization more advanced and mature than ours."

"It is the only rational assumption, do you not think? Have we not advanced, become more cultured, since the days of darkness following the Fall of Rome?" The Baron asked.

"Certainly, Baron. Outside of slaughtering each other over religious differences."

"Ah, well, you see, you prove my point. In my time, we no longer make war over religious differences—we make war over trade! An obvious improvement! But now, I propose we consider what Mars and its inhabitants are like in three categories: The inhabitants themselves. Their architecture. And inventions, machines, and such. You go first!"

"Ahhhh," Cyrano said and stretched to bide time while he thought slowly in virgin territory. "I wonder, um, whether they walk upright, like us."

"Why wouldn't they?"

"We are the only animals to walk upright on Earth, an obvious minority. Perhaps they walk on all fours?"

"Are we not the finest of all animals on Earth?"

"Certainly."

"Then walking upright is obviously the superior mode of ambulation. Why would the mature Martians be in retrograde? But, at the same time, why would they be stuck ambulating like their younger brothers, we? I suggest that they float."

"Float?"

"Gentilly from place to place as they contemplate the great questions. Or speedily if time is of the essence. I think they do this in a seated position, their legs crossed and their arms resting on small clouds they manufacture for this purpose."

"So you see the Martians as having at least the same appendages we have? Legs and arms?"

"Certainly. What could be more practical and utilitarian than our four major appendages? Five for males, of course, but we need not go into that."

"I disagree, Baron. I will be quite interested to see how the Martians procreate. And whether love is involved?"

Hieronymus Karl Friedrich, Freiherr von Münchhausen, looked quite aghast. "Do not be *über*-French, my friend. I believe Martians have left all messy interpersonal relations behind. Possibly they do not have sex differences at all. Think of the time that would save! I believe Martians are divided biologically only into classes."

"Like we are?"

"No, no, not like we are. Classes of kind, not of position. I believe there will be the Thinkers, the Doers, the Adventurers. And the Know-nothings, the Do-nothings, and the Unadventurous."

"Oh. Like we are?" Cyrano asked rhetorically as his smile indicated that he was silently saying, *Touche!*

"Humph!" heaved out of the Baron. "Architecture! What do you think Martian buildings will be like?"

"Wondrous structures, I suppose."

"Exactly!" The Baron said, excited that he and Cyrano might be sharing a vision here. "Made out of luminous organic materials and in colors never seen by the eye of man."

"But, red—

"Ah, yes, you are right! Colors in variations of red, then, never seen by the eye of man!"

"And tall?"

"Of course, tall, very tall buildings. Intelligent beings always reach higher and higher. And as they can float, there is no limit to how high they can go."

"And the buildings connected by, oh, let us call them sky bridges when the Martians would prefer to saunter instead of float."

"Marvelous! Yes! Now you are wondering well!" The Baron said, not understanding the slight satire of Cyrano's suggestion.

"And what of Martian inventions and machines, Baron?"

"Sailing ships that provide their own wind. Machines that create artificial heat in the winter and sweet, soft cool breezes in the summer. Clothes that repel all dirt and stains, thus never need to be washed. A small, tiny, minuscule machine that surreptitiously picks your nose for you. That will be handy for both you and I, eh, Cyrano? Beds that recreate the conditions inside your mother's womb allowing one to get a decent night's sleep. A machine that swats insects with a sound irritating to them but pleasant to people. Clothes that protect you against the elements, but weigh next to nothing, look fabulous, and never bunch up in dark secret places."

"Wonders!" Cyrano exclaimed, genuinely impressed and awestruck over the heights of the Baron's imagination. "Absolute wonders! What people! What architecture! What inventions! What wonders await us on Mars! But, Baron, what about Mars itself? The landscape."

"The landscape, yes, yes, we must consider the landscape. Surely whereas our Earth is dominated by blue, green, and brown, Mars must be dominated by reds, pinks, and rust. The Martian trees, for example. I see red, translucent trunks with translucent pink leaves."

"Why translucent, Baron?"

"It is obvious, my dear Cyrano. Mars is farther from the Sun than Earth. Sunshine then is weaker. After Martian trees have gathered what benefits they need from the Sun, their translucence allows the residue sunshine to pass to the ground to benefit other creatures. Also, as our leaves turn yellow and red with colder weather, I believe Martian leaves will first turn a light green then darken to an intense deep blue, like lapis lazuli."

"That should be stunning to see."

"Absolutely!"

"Do you think there will be great oceans on Mars?" Cyrano asked, thinking perhaps, about childhood days at the seashore.

"Without a doubt."

"How can you be so sure?"

"Where else can they sail their great auto-wind ships?"

"Ah. And great rivers like the Seine?"

"Yes! Flowing down from all the magnificent mountains, every one of them pink snow-capped. Remember, being farther from the Sun, Mars in the winter gets much colder."

"And what about deserts, Baron? Will there be vast stretches of near-lifeless deserts on Mars?"

"Cyrano, my friend, try to take our musing seriously. But, of course, there will be no deserts on Mars. The Martians are far advanced, they would allow not even one hectare of their home to be anything but verdant. Or possibly I should say, *rouge-ant*?"

"Yes, I suppose that follows," Cyrano acknowledged. "But something is bothering me, my dear Baron."

"Pray, tell?"

"You have been waxing quite enthusiastically about the details of Mars, but with your power to lie things into exis-tence, are you not possibly bringing them about?"

"No, no, my dear sir! Not at all. You see, to lie effectively, you must first know the truth. Since we do not yet know the truth but only speculate, there is no danger for me, with my superior imagination and perceptive abilities, to alter reality."

Cyrano simply nodded at the Baron's declaration, and the Great Munchausen began to consider all the various non-intelligent Martian creatures that might populate the red and pink landscape.

The Baron talked and talked for a duration that may have been long or may have been short or somewhere in between. There was no way to tell as the chariot of Queen Mab contained no timepieces, and they certainly could not tell by the daily track of Sun and moon. The only punctuation in the flow of time and talk was when the Baron became hungry and would lie up some German delicacies for himself and French ones for Cyrano. The limits to the Baron's abilities became clear to Cyrano when he discovered to his dismay that the Baron's imagination of French cuisine never quite got the sauces right. But Cyrano, being a gentleman, would never have said a word about it to the Baron, assuming he could have gotten a word in edgewise to have done so.

5

CYRANO DE BERGERAC AND
BARON MUNCHAUSEN ON MARS

"We are here!" Baron Munchausen exclaimed with ex-citement and a non-Teutonic giddiness.

"How do you know?" Cyrano rightly asked.

"We have landed. We have stopped. There is no move-ment."

"I have felt no movement since leaving Earth."

"I am not used to being doubted, Cyrano!" The Baron said with very Teutonic umbrage.

"My apologies, my dear Baron, I do not mean to offend."

"Already forgotten, my friend. Please open the coach door and let us introduce ourselves to Mars!"

"Ah, Baron, one moment before I do that."

"Yes, yes?" The Baron anxiously wanted to get on with it.

"Since it may be colder on Mars than we are used to. And since we have no idea if the Martians breathe the same air we breathe. Would it not be prudent for you to lie up a surrounding bubble of our native atmosphere?"

The Baron was impressed. "A fine idea, Savinien Cyrano de Bergerac. And to think you have not even begun your philosophical studies yet. So, I extend this bubble out, oh, say, one-quarter of a kilometer. Now let us see Mars!"

Cyrano opened the coach door, and the two gentlemen exited the chariot of Queen Mab and looked around.

In complete synchronization, each man's mouth slowly opened until their jaws allowed no more mobility. And, as if connected in a dance, each man's eyes widened beyond believing. When it came to voice, only the Baron managed to speak.

"Well—this is a disappointment."

Stretching out before them was a reddish expanse of a desert under a light pink sky. Cyrano and the Baron saw no life anywhere. No life at all, animal, vegetable, or even mineral. There were no structures, no buildings, not even anthills. Nothing intelligent floated in the air, nor did anything dumb. All they saw was the rusty earth of Mars laid out before them with various tracks along the ground as if giants had scratched them. And with barren mountains off in the distance. And rocks, rocks, and rocks scattered in no discernible logical manner all along the ground.

"Is it possible that this is but one geographic feature of Mars?" Cyrano asked. "That Mars does indeed have deserts, and we just happened to have landed in one? And that the civilized portion of the planet with fabulous architecture and wonderful floating people are elsewhere?"

"Yes, yes, my friend. Back into the chariot of Queen Mab!"

The Baron then lied them to a multitude of longitudes and latitudes. But, upon opening the coach door at each location, they could see only slight variations of the original landscape in which they had landed.

The Baron was inconsolable.

"Time to go home, I think," Cyrano said to Hieronymus Karl Friedrich, Freiherr von Münchhausen.

"Yes, I agree. But it is hard to lie when you have faced the truth."

"What, surely not for you! You said—

"Knowing the truth is not the same as facing the truth.

"But you are *Lügenbaron*! You were *Lügenbaron* before we came to Mars, and you will be *Lügenbaron* for a long time after."

The Baron looked upon the young cavalier before him. A handsome young man, despite his nose. The Baron smiled and waved his right hand in a circular motion. The nine postillion monkey-sized crickets goaded the nine bulls forward faster and faster until the lead bull made his incredible leap. Then, they were off, streaking away from the disappointing red planet.

6

THE RETURN TO EARTH

After experiencing the flattening of escaping Mars' gravity—a diminished experience compared to breaking away from Earth's gravity, but uncomfortable nevertheless—Cyrano and the Baron settled themselves for the journey home.

Cyrano sat upright and quietly focused his interior attention on all he had seen on Mars. Trying his best to memorize all the views of all the landscapes they had experienced. They were all quite similar, but with enough differences to give each one a hint of uniqueness. It was mentally cataloging this uniqueness that occupied Cyrano. And, oddly, these slight variations in barrenness thrilled Cyrano.

The Baron, though, seemed to have given up his Baronness. He slumped into his seat and took on a woeful continence to rival the great Quixote as he rested his head onto the palm of one hand.

Cyrano was concerned. Where was the confident, prideful, gloriously inflated Baron he had come to know in this deflated man before him? "My dear Baron, please, do not become *découragé*. We have gone somewhere and seen something no other humans on Earth in your time or mine have ever gone to or seen. We are the greatest of explorers, the exclusive holders of truth! We must now return to Earth and report what we have seen to the world. We will travel the globe, speaking before every society of natural philosophers in each nation that has one. They will be amazed! They will be thrilled! They will bestow so many honors on us we will have to build a warehouse to hold them!"

Despite Cyrano's enthusiasm, the Baron was unmoved. He looked up at Cyrano from his slumped position and hand-hammocked head. Then, while sighing, he slowly raised his head as upright as he could tolerate it. "*Au contraire,* as you French like to say along the Seine, we will be bestowed with curses and condemnations and cries of 'Off with their heads!'"

"Baron Munchausen! You do not mean that!"

"I do, my dear Cyrano, I certainly do. Someday, Man will want to know, indeed, need to know the facts about Mars that we have discovered. I predict that. But how will they ever get to that position without first having the wonder of speculation? The inspiration for imagining? The lies that lead to truth? Do we not tell children lies first to prepare them for realities? No, no, my dear Cyrano, we must continue to lie to the children of Earth. To fill them with that questing spirit, that forward motion to get there themselves, to see for themselves. If we tell them that Mars is nothing but a big, empty, and quite dirty rock, they will just say, 'Oh, okay, what's for supper?' No, better, we should fill their heads with the amazement they desire until they can handle the facts they require. So, as for me, I will continue to conjure, to spin tales, to lie. I suggest you do the same."

It is not accurate to say that Cyrano was shocked by what the Baron said. He wanted to be and tried to be, but just could not be. The wisdom of the Baron's statement seemed much too clear to him.

"And Savinien Cyrano de Bergerac..."

"Yes, Baron."

"Study your philosophy and write. And do compose your *Voyage to the Moon*. It will be good. Oh, just a small step, of course, but certainly foreshadowing giant leaps. But, if I may make one small suggestion, hopefully without altering the future."

"I would be honored, Baron Munchausen."

"You will come up with several clever ways to fly to the moon. Using bottled captured dew that rises in the early morning sun, for example. And magnets! And such other ways. They are not as imaginative as this great chariot of Queen Mab, of course, but clever. However, one of them, an idea of attaching rockets to a machine to go off in stages and then drop back to Earth one after the other— that's a much too absurd idea even for me! I would not embarrass yourself with that one."

When they returned to Earth, the Baron lied them back in time to a moment just after they had left. They exited the chariot of Queen Mab to stand on the lonely country road by Cyrano's cypress tree. As the hazelnut coach faded from existence, Cyrano, feeling exhausted, staggered to his tree and sat with his back against it. He was ashamed of himself, he wanted to bid a gracious farewell with a deep flourished bow to Baron Munchausen, but he just couldn't stand. As his eyes drooped, demanding to shut, Cyrano managed to keep them open long enough to see the Baron's magnificent head slowly fade, allowing the moon to reappear and dominate. Cyrano's eyes finally fully closed as he muttered, "Rockets?"

Cyrano was still under his cypress tree when the sun was just rising, still in a deep sleep and snoring. It was a subtle, musical snore, almost flute-like in sound given his long, luxurious nose. It rose up into the air and joined the many lilting, lovely songs of early birds out looking for worms.

FROM STAGE TO PAGE

THE PHASES OF MADE ON THE MOON

An Essay

I first published this essay on my blog, The Emotional Rationalist, in 2019. I have made some minor revisions for its inclusion here.

I started writing *Made on the Moon*, a story of a little man obsessed with the moon, in the mid-1970s. I was, at that time, writing articles and reviews for *Neworld Magazine*, an arts publication of the Inner City Cultural Center in Los Angeles. The ICCC was an exciting and inspiring place to work with its complex of theaters, dance spaces, and galleries housed in an old Masonic lodge.

I don't know if there were old Masonic ghosts there, but there were plenty of living actors, dancers, visual artists, and writers running around with purpose, doing essential training and work, many of whom went on to award-winning careers.

Made on the Moon started out as a short story pretending to be a journalist's Q&A interview with the story's protagonist, Stanley Lewis, an old man of querulous nature. He informs the journalist that he had wanted to go to the moon from the time he was an infant. An unusual ambition for one that young, I think you'll agree. The story takes place sometime in the near future, over a hundred years from Stanley's birth in 1949.

Like his creator, Stanley turned out to be a loquacious chap when talking about his life, and the piece soon became more a monologue than a Q&A. Since the ICCC had a program of giving readings of plays, I decided to turn *Made on the Moon* into a one-man play. But it didn't quite work—questions needed to be asked of Stanley. So I put the journalist back, and it became a two-character play.

Eventually, the journalist morphed into three mysterious yet very individual interviewers asking questions of Stanley for an unrevealed purpose. They gave the play a rounder, more theatrical feel. And allowed me to go deeper into Stanley's stories of his life, both those mundanely true and those pure rocket-powered flights of fancy.

I don't remember where I was in Stanley's story when I stopped working on it as other activities started to dominate my time. First, I got involved in writing for *The Cinemaphile,* a start-up film newspaper. That led to a job as Executive Secretary of ASIFA-Hollywood, an animation society of professionals and fans. Which led to becoming a programmer specializing in animation for the 1978 Los Angeles International Film Exposition, or Filmex.

After that year's exposition, I left Filmex (although I was a guest programmer for several years) to set up a one-man publicity shop. I specialized in animation clients, including Chuck Jones, Bill Melendez, and Richard Williams. Which led to my wanting to produce animation features. That ambition led to getting involved with a very young Brad Bird and *Star Wars* producer Gary Kurtz to develop an animation project. Which led to my joining Gary's company, which led to a year in Tokyo on a joint American/Japanese animated feature. Although it was a period of intense activity, I still made time for personal writing. But I had switched to working on a novel, leaving the unfinished

Made on the Moon in a file cabinet.

I left Gary's company in the summer of 1984 but stayed in Tokyo for a few months of quiet time to finish my novel. Once home, and once my wife Amanda and I were re-settled in Los Angeles, I got back to work on *Made on the Moon*. I didn't get far, though. I got stuck, as will happen, and didn't know where to next take Stanley's story. Much of what I had written was semi-autobiographical. But what was to come, which was to take Stanley years into the future, well past his 100th birthday, being unwritten in my own life was unavailable as inspiration. Besides, I didn't intend to map the rest of Stanley's life based on the hoped-for geography of my own. I had far more weirdly interesting and nicely nefarious, yet vague, incidents in mind for him. It was just getting them out of mind and onto paper that was the problem.

I stopped writing this time at the point in the story where Stanley had become an unhappy high school teacher. Which, by the way, is not autobiographical—but might have been. Possibly, because of this, I didn't quite know where to take Stanley next. Then on the morning of January 28th, 1986, I was coming out of the shower when Amanda called out to tell me that the Challenger space shuttle was about to launch. I wrapped a robe around myself and went to the living room to see the launch. I loved watching giant rocket launches sending brave professional explorers into space. I had ever since the Mercury program. This love was, indeed, part of the core of *Made on the Moon*.

It was a love that had grown out of the rocket launches of imagination in science fiction films, which I had watched with wide-eyed anticipation.

But this launch was different from all previous launches. The first civilian was being shot into space—a teacher. A historic launch, then, and not to be missed.

The launch became tragically, horribly historic when 73 seconds into its flight, the Challenger broke apart, killing everyone on board, including the teacher, Christa McAuliffe.

It was a shock. It was deeply, painfully sad. And yet, I now knew what the next scene in *Made on the Moon* had to be. I immediately went to my desk and recreated what I had just seen from the point of view of Stanley. I had him watch the tragedy unfold along with some very dull, uninterested high school students in the Social Studies class he was teaching. After that, the rest of the play flowed easily into Stanley's very particular and peculiar future.

Writers are vampires. You do have to understand that. We suck the blood of our experiences and the experiences of others, good or bad, joyful or tragic, whatever serves the needs of storytelling.

I was still involved in Hollywood, trying to develop my own projects, sometimes working for film companies in various capacities. But whenever I could promote a production or even a reading of *Made on the Moon*, I would do so. I was pleased with it and felt that it would play well on stage. But if you think filmmaking is hard, try getting a play produced, especially in Los Angeles. But, nevertheless, *Made on the Moon* had some readings by actors who liked it a lot, and they were always encouraging. But no fully staged production came about.

In 1990 I became the president of Chuck Jones Productions. In 1992, I formed my own company with a partner. We secured a two-picture deal at MGM and sold a project to Columbia. Then, in 1995, Warner Bros tapped us to produce the animation for *Space Jam*, the Michael Jordan/Bugs Bunny multi-million-dollar marketing attempt to extend the life, especially in toys, of the old Looney Tunes characters.

Work on *Space Jam* took me to London several times to consult with animation studios that we contracted to work on the film. I met an energetic, intelligent, young production assistant at one of the studios, Pippa Ford, who shared my love of theater and wanted to work in it. I gave her *Made on the Moon* to read. She loved it and organized some young British actors to stage it at the 1996 Edinburgh Fringe Festival for three weeks. It received a four-star review in *The Scotsman*. I don't remember the review in total, but I do remember it said that the play "...would not be dismissed from the stage." Which meant, I think, that the reviewer appreciated it as a fully theatrical work of art.

Amanda and I and our young daughter, Miranda, went over to Edinburgh for the final week of the run. It was, as you might imagine, a wonderful experience.

We returned to Los Angeles, hoping that *Made on the*

Moon would have more productions in the U.K., but, alas, that never happened.

In 1998 Amanda heard of a play-reading program at the Coronet Theater in L.A. and suggested I submit *Made on the Moon*. I did so, and they picked it up immediately. The director cast comedian/actor Paul Provenza in the role of Stanley. I was thrilled from the first table read—Paul played Stanley exactly as Stanley had always played in my head. It was a very successful reading. After that, Paul decided to secure a production of the play for him to star in. He sent it out to a lot of theater people he had worked with. Eventually, a producer in New York who loved Paul decided to produce a limited run of MOTM in an off-Broadway theater on 45th Street in midtown Manhattan.

Just as things were about to start on this production, Paul got cast in a new Showtime series, *Beggars & Choosers*. Unfortunately, it was beginning production almost immediately in Vancouver and Paul had to leave. Without Paul, the producer pulled out. It was deeply disappointing. But then I didn't want to do it without Paul, either.

After *Beggars & Choosers* ended, Paul kept trying to get a production of *Made on the Moon* going. However, his career was taking different turns, and nothing ever came together.

I put *Made on the Moon* aside. And I started writing novels again in 1993. By 2003 I saw the publication of *Blood is Pretty: The First Fixxer Adventure*, my satiric Hollywood thriller. Since then, I have had nine more novels published in various genres and a book of essays about my friend and colleague, the great Ray Bradbury.

Made on the Moon resurfaced once more in 2009 when I directed a staged reading of the play at the Writers Guild of America. I was thrilled to have two *Star Trek* doctors in the cast, John Billingsley from *Star Trek: Enterprise* and Robert Picardo from *Star Trek: Voyager*. John played Stanley wonderfully, bringing a voice to him different from the one in my head, but one that was absolutely right. And is now the one in my head. Robert was delicious as the leader of the interviewers. The second interviewer was the very talented and funny Bonita Friedericy, a regular on the TV series *Chuck*. The third was played by Johanna McKay, who later became a professor in the Theater department at Los Angeles City College.

It was a great reading and a fantastic night. And some interest in a fully staged production of *Made on the Moon* was discussed, but, as seemed to be this play's fate, it came to nothing. I guess the reviewer in Edinburgh had been wrong. *Made on the Moon* was constantly being dismissed from the stage.

In the great joy I've had writing novels for more than twenty years now, I've come to realize that my one true passion is for writing narrative prose. As much as I love film and theater, the art of prose is what thrills me the most. So thinking about this one day, I decided to rewrite *Made on the Moon* in narrative prose.

The material, which runs just ninety minutes on stage, did not justify adapting *Made on the Moon* as a novel. But it was just the right length for a novella. In making the adaptation, I believe I lost none of the piece's power on the stage. And it allowed me to add scenes and deepen emotions. I was happy with the narrative sections I wrote. After I finished, I realized that *Made on the Moon* may now be in its perfect form. Which makes sense because, as a play script, it almost always got the universal response of, "This is a *great* read!" Not all plays are, essentially being blueprints for staging. *Made on the Moon* has had a trip almost as far as one to the moon and back. But I think it has finally found a home.

WHAT I WOULD PUT ON MY WIKIPEDIA PAGE IF I THOUGHT WIKIPEDIA WOULD LET ME

A WackiWiki

Generally speaking, writers like to write, but they hate to market. And yet, in this 21st Century we are encouraged to do so. The philosophy being, if you don't thump your own tub, no one else will. This being the case it is often suggested that a writer should have a Wikipedia page to help spread their "brand." Having a brand is a concept I abhor, but I do see the logic behind it. I once tried to come up with a text for a potential Wikipedia page for myself. Unfortunately the satiric writer in me supplanted the logical marketeer, and the following is all I could come up with.

S teven Paul Leiva is an American novelist who once led a secret life in Hollywood. He was born at The Woman's Hospital in Pasadena, California, on May 26, 1949, shortly before noon. It was just like him to show up for lunch. Soon after his birth, they razed The Woman's Hospital and put a parking lot in its place. It has never been firmly established if the two events were related.

At the age of three and a half, Leiva's family moved to the city of Azusa, just east of Pasadena, where he grew up. The city's motto was "Everything from A to Z in the USA." The motto was not wholly accurate.

Levia attended Azusa High School, a well-funded school due to the taxes paid by businesses in Azusa that brewed beer, concocted friction proofing, and built rockets. It has never been firmly established if the three were related.

While attending Azusa High, Leiva fell in with the wrong crowd—the Drama Department and its Aztec Players troupe of actors. Leiva loved acting. But upon graduation, he discovered that he wasn't six feet tall (as his mother had always promised he would be). And so, traveling under the false assumption that all actors had to be six feet tall, Leiva gave up the idea of acting and decided to write instead. He figured you didn't need to be tall to write as you usually sat when you did it.

Right out of high school, as the war in Vietnam was heating up, Leiva enlisted in the Air Force as a way to avoid the draft. It was a counterintuitive idea, if not downright ironic. However, after a career of twenty-two days, Leiva was discharged due to a discharge from a cyst in a sensitive place. It wasn't quite as glamorous and protest-y as moving to Canada, but it did the trick.

Back home, Leiva enrolled in the local community college (then embarrassingly known as a junior college) to see if he could learn a thing or two. Some colleges are named after great men or women, or the major urban area they are located in. His college was named after fruit. Nevertheless, Leiva did learn a thing or two at Citrus College and was grateful to do so.

From Citrus College, Leiva left Azusa to continue his fruity education in Orange County. He entered the hollow halls of a state college (later, it grew up and became a state university). He soon left those hollow halls when he found himself unable to suppress chuckling at professors who professed that they were *not* living a pristine, un-real-world Ivory Tower existence because they actually drove to work on the freeway. (Yes, Leiva didn't get it, either). There was also the fact that he was now married with his first child. So he left the college *summa come-to-poppa* and entered the world of retail (which is most definitely not an ivory tower existence).

Leiva became a major appliance salesman of very minor talent. He was happy to help people purchase appliances they wanted. But had an aversion to talking them into refrigerators and stoves they didn't want. Silly him.

Leiva consoled himself with writing short stories. He found —as he suspected he would—that the landscaping of blank pages with little black letters forming words forming sentences forming paragraphs forming characters, ideas, causes and effects was not only fun but possibly nourishing. He left retail.

Or, to be honest, retail left him. Much like his marriage had a few months before.

Set adrift in a no-income real world with nary an ivory tower to be found, Leiva scanned the Help Wanted pages of the *Los Angeles Times*. His eyes fell eagerly onto HELP WANTED: ADVERTISING SALESMAN FOR AN ARTS MAGAZINE. YOUR INTEREST IN THE ARTS MORE IMPORTANT THAN YOUR ABILITY TO SELL.

Perfect! As Leiva had a deep interest in the arts and absolutely no ability to sell.

Leiva went in for an interview and learned that it was a commission-only job. He was disappointed. There was something about a counted-upon paycheck that he had grown accustomed to. However, the editor of the magazine—a perfectly lovely man who unfortunately dressed like a pimp—having been informed of the circumstances of Leiva's separation from his last job, told Leiva to file for unemployment. "Around here, we call unemployment, government support of the arts."

And so Leiva filed for unemployment and strived to sell ad space in the magazine with little, or possibly minuscule, success. Still, the editor saw something in Leiva and gave him a shot at writing articles and reviews for the magazine. Leiva was uncompensated for the work, but it was still damn nice of the editor. Leiva happily landscaped some blank pages with pieces on art, books, beauty, and joy.

But there was a dark cloud on the horizon. It was called Hollywood. Not the photographic, flashy Hollywood of glamorous stars and larger-than-life producers and directors, and couches to cast upon, and craft services to get fat on. But the hand-drawn Hollywood of cartoons (sometimes thought of as animation—when they were thought of at all). It was a secret world of adherents and acolytes with code words and knowing nods. Leiva found himself recruited into a cartoon cult. There were strange initiation rites and hazing. He was sometimes forced to wear no pants, stuff his five-fingered hands into four-fingered gloves, and speak in a funny voice. Funny ha-ha *and* funny weird. There were cult leaders of one-syllable names and enforcers who drew the line and demanded you always be "on model."

Once again, Leiva consoled himself by landscaping blank pages with little black letters forming words forming sentences forming paragraphs forming characters, ideas, causes and effects. But this time, he was writing novels. As he suspected he would, he found that it was not only fun but possibly life-saving.

After nearly twenty years in the cartoon cult, Leiva rose to a high position and was given a "plum" mission. He was tasked to help facilitate the pairing of wacky, crazy, dare we say, looney cartoon illusions-of-life (anthropomorphic in the main) with fast dribbling, high jumping, and often sweaty, taller-than-normal actual-life. Ironically this afforded Leiva the opportunity to escape the cult when a tunnel formed between the worlds of the illusion-of-lifers and the actual-lifers.

He made his break, crawling as fast as he could through the tunnel, careful to avoid the monsters and creatures dwelling within. Once thought mythical, Leiva had discovered that they were all too real. With cunning and stealth, Leiva slipped past the Flaming Egos (although he did get singed). He slid unseen under the feet of the Prancing Primadonnas (boy, could they dance!). And he managed to stay under the radar of the Tiny Meanie Caustic Clueless Executors (whose wild calls of NO! never stopped reverberating). Luckily Leiva was ignored by the Dark Digital Demons streaming *en masse* through the tunnel. They were heading to the illusion-of-life land to suck the pencil lead out of the weak, defenseless cartoons and replace it with zeros and ones.

But Leiva didn't care. He broke out of the tunnel and into the sunshine, free! Free to be he and him! Hand-in-hand with his second wife and second child and occasionally his visiting first child (all adored), Leiva found an open and vast world of blank pages. Beautiful blank pages he could landscape with little black letters forming words forming sentences forming paragraphs forming characters, ideas, causes, and effects. Leiva was finally happy. It has been firmly established that the two events were related.

ABOUT THE AUTHOR

Before publishing ten critically acclaimed works of fiction, award-winning and Amazon Bestselling author Steven Paul Leiva spent more than twenty years in the entertainment industry as a writer and producer. He worked with such talent as Academy Award-winning producer Richard Zanuck; producer-director Ivan Reitman; literary legend and screenwriter Ray Bradbury; Star Wars producer Gary Kurtz; Looney Tunes legend Chuck Jones; manager/producer Ken Kragen, and Animation Feature Academy Award-winning director Brad Bird. He even lent his voice to the Academy Award shortlisted (placing in the top ten) animated short, "The Indescribable Nth."

Leiva was a producer of animation for *Space Jam*, putting together an ad hoc animation studio for Warner Bros and executive producer Ivan Reitman in three days.

During this time, he wrote novels and a play, *Made on the Moon*, which premiered at the Edinburgh Festival Fringe, receiving a four-star review from *The Scotsman*.

After *Space Jam*, Leiva decided to concentrate on writing novels. Since 2003 he has published nine novels, a novella, and a book of essays.

His work has been praised by literary great Ray Bradbury, Oscar-winning film producer Richard Zanuck, *New York Times* Bestselling author and Pulitzer Prize finalist Diane Ackerman, and Star Trek actor John Billingsley, the greatest bookworm in Hollywood. He has received the Scribe Award from the International Association of Media Tie-in Writers.

You can find Steven on Facebook, Twitter @StevenPaul-Leiva, and he muses and on occasion amuses at http://emotionalrationalist. blogspot.com/.

ALSO BY STEVEN PAUL LEIVA

Fiction

Blood is Pretty: The First Fixxer Adventure

Hollywood is an All-volunteer Army: The Second Fixxer Adventure

Traveling in Space

The 12 Dogs of Christmas: A Novelization

By the Sea: A Comic Novel

IMP: A Political Fantasia

Made on the Moon: A Novella

Journey to Where: A Contemporary Scientific Romance

Creature Feature: A Horrid Comedy

Bully 4 Love: A Rather Odd Love Story

Made on the Moon: A Play

Non-Fiction

Searching for Ray Bradbury: Writings about the Writer and the Man

Made in the USA
Middletown, DE
23 November 2021

53235656R00120